THE RELUCTANT ADVENTURES

OF

FLETCHER CONNOLLY

ON THE

INTERSTELLAR RAILROAD

VOLUME 3

BANJAXED CEILI

F. R. SAVAGE

THE RELUCTANT ADVENTURES OF FLETCHER
CONNOLLY ON THE INTERSTELLAR RAILROAD
VOLUME 3
BANJAXED CEILI

First published in the United States of America in 2016 by Knights Hill Publishing.

Cover art by Christian Bentulan
Interior design and layout by Felix R. Savage

ISBN-10:1-937396-22-3
ISBN-13:978-1-937396-22-0

THE RELUCTANT ADVENTURES

OF

FLETCHER CONNOLLY

ON THE

INTERSTELLAR RAILROAD

VOLUME 3

BANJAXED CEILI

CHAPTER 1

Seventh Heaven is hotter than hell, Arcadia is a mafiosi-infested version of Silicon Valley with bad lighting, and Shangri-La might be nice if it were not for the dinosaur-analogs. There's no truth in advertising when it comes to the names that mischievous and spiteful explorers have bestowed on the habitable planets of the Milky Way.

Treetop is the rare exception. Coming off the Railroad on an interstellar shuttle, all I see from the window is treetops.

They're amazing, these trees. They grow twelve *miles* tall. Their flat dark-green canopies poke up into the stratosphere, like clusters of green fried eggs with dessicated edges.

You can't breathe up there, so the owners of the trees have built various pressurized structures to serve as parking garages. We swoop down towards an equatorially located tree with glinting bubbles dotting its leaf pads like raindrops.

I never expected to see this sight for myself in real life. I'm not rich enough. Yet here I am.

Between the trees, I glimpse Treetop's dark mucky surface, a long, *long* way down.

1

The shuttle lands on a leaf pad near one of the bubble-style spaceport terminals, and taxis at high speed towards the silvery dome. Is it? Can it be? The dome comes nearer and nearer on my seatback screen. Everyone else squeals, impressed, as we shoot straight in through the wall. I grit my teeth. The dome is a force field—the very latest, priciest thing. Keeps air in, lets solid objects in and out if they're moving fast enough. *I* discovered force fields last year, on the Omega Centauri spur.

Well, to be completely honest, my uncle Finian discovered them, and a heap of other pirates were onto them, as well. But *I* found out how they're made, and I could have claimed the discovery and auctioned it off for billions, if everything hadn't gone tits-up at the last minute.

So the patent went to Samsung. And obviously, they've already made some sales to early adopters, such as the owners of 12-mile-high trees.

Never mind. He who laughs last laughs best.

And after tonight I will be richer than any Big Tech executive, without the bother of running a company, either.

At the thought of the hazards ahead, nervous anticipation stabs me. I stand up and follow the other party-goers off the shuttle.

We step down onto rugged leaf-stuff, in what seems to be open space, with only a silvery glimmer at the horizon to reassure you that there's something holding in the air. Overhead floats Treetop's full moon, mottled like blue cheese. Just below the moon, the Interstellar Railroad bisects the sky. It looks like a thin black band against the golden evening.

Every habitable planet in the Milky Way has a loop of the

Railroad around it. Earth got one in 2024, the year of my own birth, as it happens. We figured out how to use it quite quickly, given that there are no living aliens left in the galaxy to show us how—and since then it's been one mad scramble for the treasures that the aliens all left behind when they went extinct. Treetop is one of those treasures, a jewel that's long outlived its previous owners.

The air inside the forcefield dome is on the warm side, oxygen-rich, laced with exhaust fumes from the shuttle buses, taxis, and flying cars standing around. I'm already starting to sweat inside my costume.

A flight attendant hands me a four-way leash. "Your pets, my lord. Gosh, they're so cute!" She stoops to pet one of the treecats. True to form, the vicious little creature bites her. She pulls back with a cry of pain.

My instinct is to say something like 'I hope you've had your booster shot recently,' but I've got to stay in character. I sniff, grab the leash, and stalk away, following dozens of party guests dressed as aliens.

It had to be a bloody fancy dress party.

The silver lining, though, is no one's going to recognize me in the costume I have on.

Not that they'd recognize me anyway. I am a nobody, and these are filthy-rich stackers. They've had all the advantages of assortative marriage, embryo screening, prenatal DNA optimization, early-childhood enrichment classes, private schools, plutocratic networks, chips implanted in their brains are the newest thing, and it's a safe bet that every man-purse, handbag, oversized codpiece, and iPhone holster in sight holds a stash of nootropic drugs to keep their brains performing at three times normal human capacity.

And all these highly intelligent people have persuaded themselves it is a fine idea to dress up as extinct aliens.

Some of the costumes are great, actually. In the crowd waiting for the elevator, I see a naked Pygmy Ent—they came from Cassiopeia 2c and never got off their home planet; a Silicon Person riding on a floating gravsled; three Sagittarians with horns and hooves; a group of Krells carrying their tails over their arms; and a Puzzler whose legs really look triple-jointed, how the feck's he managed that? There's also a rabble of Klingonss (so-called because you find their 500-million-year-old corpses every fecking place) and Denebites (four arms, beaky faces, very easy to dress up as).

I'm relieved to see that I'm not the only person with living accessories. The Sagittarians each have a flock of little birds perching on their horns, some of the Klingonss are carrying tribbles (the latest alien pet fad!) and the Silicon Person has a human slave in a jewelled bikini, chained hand and foot, with a black bag over her head. Bet she's cold.

"Baron Short!"

That's me.

I turn, languidly, and my beak rides up over my left eye.

Yes, of course I'm dressed as a Denebite. It was the cheapest costume.

Through my watering right eye, I make out what appears to be a lean, medium-height human male.

"Ah, Short, my old chum!"

He strides through the crowd. I'm relieved to have someone to talk to, so I don't look such a friendless wally. But I wish he'd drop the fake British accent. I'm Irish, and we're supposed to be friends.

I adjust my beak to say, "Is that your costume? Because it looks like you're wearing a tuxedo."

"The name's Bond. James Bond."

I suppose Sam does look a bit like the new Bond, that Moroccan fella. In reality he is the son of a notorious female pirate. He ran out on his mum when my uncle Finian was about to give her a beating. This proves he's got good timing. His judgment I am not so sure about. "You're supposed to be in fancy dress," I say.

"I am! I mean, come on, it's *obvious* Bond is an alien! He's been the same age for a hundred and five years!"

Sam gets a laugh for that from some Klingonss. He immediately attaches himself to them and expounds on his James Bond=alien theory. Ah, he's all right. I need to stop worrying.

We squeeze into the elevator, styrofoam falsies and painted limbs and rubber foreheads all jammed in together, and my treecats run up my legs to avoid being trampled. I end up with one on each shoulder, one clinging to my back with its six million sharp claws, and one sat on my *beak,* for feck's sake, scrabbling for purchase and steadily pulling the bloody thing off my face. I pry the treecat loose and give it a cuddle.

A Klingons, pedantically: "But all aliens are extinct. The longest-lived aliens were the Silicon People. And they're extinct now, too."

Yes, and thank God for that. The Silicon People were villainous customers, judging by the monuments they left around the place. But they're dust now. So is every other sapient species that once stalked the Milky Way, except us. Clearly God saved the best for last.

Sam: "OK, fine. I'm an alien who's found the Fountain of Youth, the Gizmo of Rejuvenation! Hee, hee."

Everyone laughs, in recognition of the fact that the so-called Gizmo of Rejuvenation is the ultimate A-tech that everyone wants to find, but nobody can, because it doesn't exist. I break out in hot prickles of sweat, and squeeze the treecat in my arms so tightly that it nips me.

Is Sam *trying* to give the game away?

Or just having fun?

Either way, I don't trust him. I wish we had left him out of it.

But we couldn't leave him out, because it was his idea to begin with. *He* had the information that got us started on this … call it what it is, what we're planning. Robbery.

My ears pop.

The elevator halts for a moment, then zooms down again.

Ten miles down.

It's not as hard on the body as you would think, because the spaceport up top is pressurized at 0.8 atmospheres, but it takes a while, even at this elevator's maximum rate of descent, which would leave a jet plane gasping. The bright side is by the time we reach the residential level, we've all gotten to know each other.

I emerge in the company of the Krells, who are charmed by my treecats. The wee bastards *do* have their points.

Sam roisters off with the Klingonss.

"See you later, Hofacker," I call out to him, through my beak.

We both bought our identities from the mob on Arcadia. It was the most expensive part of the entire operation. Baron Short and Lord Hofacker have unimpeachable digital histories going back to the year of their birth, 2024 in my case and 2041 in his. Jesus, he makes me feel old. Our titles are of the type anyone can award themselves if they've got their own planet, which we have, and no one's to know they are rentals. I've never been to mine, but I believe it's a shitehole in the Perseus arm. The minute our new identities went live, the party invitations started pouring in. Those Russian programmers are shite-hot.

"Dick! Dick, honey?"

I do suspect them of having a bit of fun with the names.

"Would you mind grabbing a drink for me? My tail kind of gets in the way," giggles one of the Krell, who has taken off her rubber head, saying she's hot.

She *is* hot, without the head on. Chinese, or maybe Japanese, with a sparkling smile.

Sidling through the throng, I take in the cavernous dimensions of this hall, or ballroom I suppose it is. Knurled wooden walls shoot up to lose themselves in shadows a quarter-mile overhead. The chandeliers float lower than that, powered by anti-grav. The orchestra is also floating on an anti-grav platform, scraping out classical music. I think of my friend Donal, who could play the fiddle better than any of these gowls—maybe not Vivaldi, but no one could give you a better jig or reel.

Donal is here, right now, trapped, as I am, in this tree. A fresh pang of fear shoots through me at the thought.

But a few drinks ease my nerves and soon I'm chatting away with my new friend, the headless Krell. She tells me how grim it is being a saleswoman. This is apparently what she does when she's not wearing an alien costume at King Zuckerberg's biannual trainspotting bash. I make up a whole history for the treecats based on the little I know about my rented planet. The craic is spoiled only by the brooding presence of a Silicon Person, who shows no signs of life other than to extend a tentacle from time to time and drag a bottle of bubbly into its pyramid through a hatch.

And on to dinner, where I feed my vat-grown organic venison to the treecats. Give me microwave fish 'n' chips any day. I've got no complaints about King Zuckerberg's booze, though. It is only when I try to kiss the headless Krell (on the cheek!) and almost poke her eye out, because I completely forgot I had a beak on me, that I realize I may have had a bit much.

Well, can you blame me? I'm about to steal the single most valuable item of A-tech in the universe. The Lord himself couldn't do this sober.

The dessert plates are being cleared away. An elderly soul rises into the air, chair and all. Jesus, it's Zuckerberg himself, one of the original tech moguls. He was around before the Railroad came to Earth. Now he's king of a dozen planets as well as this one. He rambles for a bit, while I sit smirking with disbelief that I am in the same room as him. Then he announces the winner of the fancy dress contest—Silicon Person!

The Sagittarians were robbed! Sure, that costume's only made of styrofoam. I think maybe Zuck's making some roundabout point about how true success is getting paid for doing nothing, which I concur with, but then it comes out that Silicon Person's been broadcasting a sort of one-man play the whole time, demonstrating his/her knowledge of Silicon People culture and apparently bringing tears to xeno-archaeologists' eyes all over the planet. He/she was broadcasting in the RF spectrum, so the stackers, with their always-on connections and this and that, could hear it, but I couldn't.

Well, be damned to the lot of youse, I think to myself. I'm about to get up and go to the bogs when the King concludes with, "And now, let's head upstairs and see if we can spot that train!"

The entire company rustles to its feet, nerdishly eager to be on time for the main event.

This train he's talking about is the Ghost Train, as the media calls it. Every two years it reappears in our part of the Orion arm. Mostly it just zooms past at many times the speed of light, but at certain planets it stops for a while. Treetop is one of those planets. It will arrive in a few minutes and sit on the local loop for the next day or so, looking sort of expectant, as if waiting for passengers.

Get *on* the Ghost Train? You'd have to be mad. There is no shortage of madmen of course, and various loons have boarded the Ghost Train in the past, never to be heard from again. But Zuckerberg's guests won't be joining them. They'll be observing the thing from a safe distance and taking selfies.

I'm not really interested in the Ghost Train. The galaxy is full of weird and wonderful A-tech and at some point you have to make the decision that you're not going to bother about all of it.

The piece of A-tech I'm interested in is much closer at hand.

Three floors down, in fact.

As everyone heads for the elevators and the flitter pads, I make for the bogs. I shut myself inside a stall with the treecats. Whenever someone rattles the door, I utter puking noises.

Soon all's quiet beyond. I let the treecats off their leashes.

As I peek out of the bathroom, they squirt between my feet and bound down the corridor. They've got an amazing gift of camouflage. Their fur turns colors like chameleons. They've vanished in the blink of a drunken eye.

I duck back into the bathroom, shuddering and whispering Hail Marys. This is it now, we're committed. No turning back.

Trembling with haste, I strip off my Denebite costume and ball it up, tying the floppy silicon arms around the bundle. Underneath it I'm wearing black jeans and a black polo shirt. I look like one of the waiters. But that's nothing. I've spent the last year in work gloves and a breathing mask, swinging a pick in an alien catacomb. If you think your job is shite, I'm here to tell you it could be worse. You could be working construction on Arcadia.

I bustle out of the bogs, and—

"Hey!"

It's one of Zuck's security guards. Of course there are security guards. Many of them, all 'roided up to superhuman dimensions, with earpieces and wraparound sunglasses.

"Those bathrooms are for guests."

"I was bursting," I say hopelessly.

"Fine, but I'm gonna have to inform your manager."

It's all over. We're busted.

"Can I see your ID, please," says the security guard, one hand dropping to his taser.

CHAPTER 2

"Help! Oh Jesus! *Help!*"

The cry for help comes from the ballroom. It hits the security guard like a whip. He's off as fast as he can jog, given that his thighs rub together from too many deadlifts.

I follow him, not because I want to but because I have to cross the ballroom to escape.

"Heeelllp!"

The few guests left in the ballroom laugh and shout advice. Two tables have been balanced on top of one another. On the top table stands a Klingons, while another Klingons steadies him.

He cannot quite reach Sam, who is swinging by one knee from a chandelier.

"Someone help me!"

Sam seems to be genuinely stuck. Also, the hem of his trousers is about to catch fire (they're *real* chandeliers). But I'm pretty sure he smiles, upside down, as I leg it across the ballroom.

Good old Sam! He must have seen me going into the bogs, and got ready to lay on a little diversion, James Bond style.

I shoot into the stairwell, heart going like the clappers. The security guard may recall my existence when he's extricated Sam from the chandelier, but he won't be able to do anything about it, because he didn't get my ID, because I don't have one.

Three or four floors down, I stop to get my bearings. I memorized a map of the whole tree—it's the size of a museum. In fact it *is* a museum to Zuck's taste in alien memorabilia. Queerly enough for a tech mogul, he's filled his tree with low-tech rubbish, statuary and frescoes and furniture the wrong shape to use, with here and there a busted satellite on a pedestal. But old Zuck's got a nose for the good stuff, as well. That is why we're here.

I keep expecting to hear burglar alarms. Every passing minute supports two conflicting conclusions: either we've failed, or we're getting away with it.

I hurry on through cathedral-like rooms. Stacker brats are playing laser baseball in a room full of Perseid etchings. Couples shag on dinghy-sized Sagittarian sofas. You could drop the whole of Lisdoonvarna, my hometown, into this tree, and never notice it was there.

Outside at last, crossing a branch as wide as a highway, I glimpse the real Treetop, the reason every yuppie wants to retire here someday. In the distance, sunlight dapples overlapping leaves that are so thick, they've got pits in them, and the pits brim with sparkling rainwater, so each leaf is like a lake filled with islands, or an island filled with lakes, and red and green mosses and ferns—all symbiotic with the great tree—fringe the ponds with shade. The air's alive with birdsong and the calls of monkey-analogs and squirrel-analogs.

If this were a residential development instead of a private kingdom, each leaf would have condos built into the leaves, all made of sustainably sourced bamboo and recycled plastic.

Higher up, you get more of a Southwestern vibe, with pretty little lizards running around on leaves so dry that they crack into gullies inhabited by frog-analogs.

Something for every taste, you see. Except mine. I'd rather live in bleeding Ennis, if I've got to deal with neighbors.

But at the moment I do understand the appeal, for it looks like paradise out there in the sunlight, and I'm sure I would be able to smell the leaf perfume everyone raves about if it were not for the catering plane parked on the branch close at hand, emitting the reek of chip fat.

I stride up the stairs and into a hell of steam and noise.

The caterers are doing all the washing-up on their planes, so as not to contaminate Zuck's water cycle. Dishwashers stand at a row of sinks, washing the King's priceless Perseid dinner service by hand.

The dishwasher nearest to me, white-aproned, sweat trickling out of the towel wrapped around his head, suds on one gaunt cheek, is Donal.

He's been working for this catering company, the one Zuckerberg always uses, for the last year, while I labored on Arcadia.

He used to be the captain of an exploration ship. Now he's a dishwasher living from paycheck to paycheck, and his hands are so raw from the bleach he can't play the fiddle anymore.

But soon he will be free and rich, and so will I, *if* we can pull this off. He catches my eye, and flashes me a quarter of a grin.

My heart leaps. I shove my bundled-up costume at him. "Some arsehole's spilt wine on this. Can you take it off at all?"

"Oh, wine stains are the worst," sings out the buxom dishwasher beyond Donal. "But I'll give it a try."

The second dishwasher is Harriet, Donal's girlfriend. She's been working for the catering company a scant few weeks. She waited to apply until he'd built up enough trust to get her the job. She spent the rest of the last year on Arcadia with me and Sam, and if I'm honest she had the hardest job of all. It was her task to train the treecats to steal the specific item we're after, from the specific place Sam told us about.

Jesus, the patience of that woman. I have a new respect for her now. I'd come back to our kip from a day of breaking up petrified alien bones and find her and Imogen still at it, coaxing the treecats through yet another rehearsal.

It's not the stealing part the 'cats had difficulty with. Those little beasts are natural kleptomaniacs. They can crack any lock in the known universe, be it a combination, biometric, or voice-recognition. I'd go to sleep to the sound of them imitating Zuckerberg's voice off the television. It's not canny.

No, the difficulty was training them to steal the *right* thing, instead of coming back with sparkly rubbish every time.

The *coming back* part was no problem, anyway.

Glancing down the plane, I see all four of them sat on a counter, disdainfully accepting tidbits from enthralled waiters. Like four-legged homing pigeons, they unerringly found Harriet in this labyrinth of a place. Fecking hell, if they're not intelligent, they're something very like it.

I pass my costume to Donal, who passes it to Harriet. She scrubs at the nonexistent stain. "That's a bit better," she says, and passes it back to Donal, and as I take it from his hands I feel the lumpy object inside.

Giddy with excitement, I thank them and exit the plane. I want to peek immediately but I force myself to wait until I reach the jacks.

Safely locked in a Portapotty *for staff use*—not making that mistake again—I shake out the costume.

An object resembling a five-inch iron nail falls out and skids across the floor.

I retrieve it and wipe it off with toilet paper.

The treecats did it! Those little beauties *did* it!

I am holding the Gizmo of Rejuvenation.

Now granted, it hasn't been proven safe yet, much less reverse-engineered for commercial manufacturing. But the media's been full of rumors over the last months that Zuckerberg may have found the Holy Grail of the exploration industry, and there've been blurry pictures of the Gizmo itself, and long-lens video of the lab where they've been poking and prodding it, and shots of suspiciously young-looking Zuckerberg confidants. Of course he hasn't used it himself, they say. He's too much in the public eye, and too wily an old bird to risk potential side effects.

Personally I think it's a complete load of bollocks.

But many other people are desperate to believe it.

Cackling to myself, I put my costume back on—it's a bit

damp and sudsy at this point. The Gizmo goes in a sterile resealable bag inside my fake Denebite paunch. I don't want that thing next to my skin. On the off chance it works, I'd be worried about side effects, too.

Disguised once more as Dick, Lord Short, I head across the highway bough to a leafpad where a luxury flitter stands waiting for the use of guests. "Up to the canopy! You can take the scenic route," I tell the pilot.

The bubble seals shut, and I recline on the leather seat while we spiral up around the great tree. Every hundred yards of altitude brings us to a new ecosystem, fractionally differentiated from the last. At about the three-mile mark, the whole tree is draped in something like Spanish moss. Four miles up, we catch a glimpse of the giant aphids that make those pits in the leaves. Jesus, they're ugly feckers. Each one has a handler standing ready with a cattleprod. Off our starboard wing, the neighboring tree rears like a green cliff in the warm haze.

Five miles up—the air still breathable, for Treetop's atmosphere is thicker than Earth's—we pass the employee housing. Each of King Zuckerberg's many minions has their own flat, in a maze of spindly buildings suspended between one bough and the next, connected by walkways, and I'm glad to see there is a safety net underneath the lot, with lost toys and dropped cellphones rolling around in it. Children wave to my flitter. It looks like a grand little community, and I remember the sadness I saw on Donal's face, before he realized I was there.

He wanted something like this. A new life in a new world, lightyears away from bleak oul' Lisdoonvarna.

So he poured his heart and soul into the *Skint Idjit*, and

the *Intergalactic Bogtrotter* after her, and all he's got to show for it is one broken-down old ship. And everyone we know in County Clare lost their shirts on the *Skint Idjit,* and Donal's been posting fictional updates all year, promising that they'll be made whole soon. The timestamps prove he's always posting late at night, after he gets back to the catering company's dormitory. It's not right, it's not fair, and there should be a better solution than crime, but we were fecked if we could think of one.

We *tried* playing by the rules, didn't we? And look where that got us.

I clutch the Gizmo of Rejuvenation through my costume, breathing heavily. I'm not interested in the scenic tour of King Zuck's tree anymore. I just want to get off this planet.

The Ghost Train's just arriving as I join the throng inside the bubble-terminal.

Keyed up with anticipation, the crowd lets out an undignified shout. All of them whip their phones out and video away.

It's a good thing smartphones now have built-in telescopic lenses. You can hardly see the blip on the Railroad high over our heads.

As the Ghost Train glides to a stop 8,000 miles above, I ease through the crowd, as if looking for the perfect place to take a selfie. In fact I'm looking for Sam.

Our taxi's parked on the far side of the terminal. Imogen sits on the bonnet, natty in her taxi driver's outfit, videoing the Ghost Train like everyone else.

We argued for ages about the merits of making a quick getaway vs. waiting for the shuttle. We plumped for the taxi, mainly because the shuttle is going back to Arcadia, and we do not want to go back to Arcadia. We will be cabbing it to the *Intergalactic Bogtrotter,* which Kenneth, Ruby, and Vanessa, the last members of our crew, have parked on Treetop's moon. Then we will vanish into the snowy wastes of a little planet I know, yes, the very planet I rented from the Arcadia mafia. Sly auld Fletch told them all it was in the Perseus arm. It's actually in the Orion arm, not far from here at all. We will hide there with the Gizmo, and the buyers can come to us. Much safer that way. Sam will handle the auction through his family connections.

But if I can't find him in the next few minutes, we're leaving without him, and I'll organize the auction myself. The Gizmo—strangely heavy for its size—keeps slipping out of the bottom of my paunch. I'm in a muck sweat, clutching my belly like a pregnant lady.

Security guards move through the throng, inspecting each and every face. Not sure what they hope to accomplish, since everyone's got masks on, but it is clear they're looking for someone.

This is it. They've discovered the Gizmo missing.

I pull my beak up higher, fighting panic.

Suddenly, everyone in front of me surges backwards.

For a second I think Sam's mounting another diversion. But this would be beyond his powers.

The elevator disgorges a squad of police officers in the blue and white uniforms of the newly created Near Earth Police Department. They're wearing reflective vests and visored helmets, as if they expect a riot. They wave their non-lethal electropulse laser pistols at the astonished crowd.

Jesus, the NEPD is going to hear from King Zuckerberg about this. The tech lobby said it was a mistake to create an interstellar police department, spirit of the frontier and all that libertarian bollocks, but the pols shoved it through because they'd had enough of the exploration industry raking it in without paying any taxes. With any luck, the NEPD will get its funding slashed after this.

The sheriff adjusts a microphone attached to his body armor. "Ladies and gentlemen! I apologize for this interruption! However, we have received an alert regarding a theft at this residence!"

A security guard approaches with a murderous expression. The sheriff grandly waves him aside.

"We have received a description of the suspects, and I regret to inform you they are amongst you at this moment! They are notorious criminals and may be dangerous, so ladies and gentlemen, please remain calm …"

The combination of a display of force and announcement of dastardly criminal activity—*who would dare?*—disturbs the guests exceedingly. They all stampede for their vehicles.

The sheriff takes off his helmet and wipes his brow, muttering, "For Jesus' sake, are youse the cognitive elite or not?" His microphone's still on, so his words echo around the terminal.

I let out an involuntary bark of horror

The sheriff is my uncle Finian.

I had heard things went sour for him on the Omega Centauri spur. I'd also heard that he ended up joining the newly formed NEPD. I could scarcely believe it at first. It must have been some sort of deal for him to keep out of prison. Either that, or he felt himself slowing down—he is seventy-six, after all—and jumped at the chance to spend his golden years committing violent extortion, *and* collecting a paycheck with union benefits.

His officers overtake the stampeding guests. They make a beeline for …

… someone else?

To shocked murmurs, they drag forth Silicon Person and his/her human slave.

"Ha!" booms Finian. "Your criminal career ends here, Increpit, you blackguard!"

Or here's a better theory: he's joined the NEPD to pay off old scores.

"You can't arrest me," screeches Silicon Person. "You've got the wrong man!"

"I've got you dead to rights!" Finian gloats.

Styrofoam tiles scatter. A skinny male figure rises from the ruins of Silicon Person, still wearing his broadcasting headset. Jesus, it is the infamous claim-jumper Ivan 'Stellar Increpit' Skowalski, whose face is on every top ten most wanted list on the internet.

"You're under arrest!" Finian snarls, while his minions search Increpit and his accomplice.

The scattered guests come back. The police officers are trying to get the bag off Increpit's accomplice's head, and are having trouble with the chains. Increpit is calling Finian an unreformed old pirate, Finian is shouting him down with reminders of his past illegal activities, and the party guests are falling over each other to video them—this is more exciting than the boring old Ghost Train, is it not? I would like to stop and stare myself, but caution prevails. I sidle through the fringes of the crowd, heading for Imogen's taxi. She's standing on the bonnet, watching the fun. "Jesus,

Imogen," I mutter under my breath, "get down off there before he recognizes you!"

The police officers finish searching Increpit and his accomplice. "Sir, um, it's not on them."

"I told you, I told you!" yells Increpit.

"Ah, you cunt," Finian says. "Well, there *was* a theft …"

"We won best costume!" Increpit shouts. We've done nothing wrong!"

"Yeah, well you have done on other occasions," says Finian, rallying. "Cuff them," he snarls, and I think if this is how the NEPD is going to go on, I hope it gets defunded pronto.

Increpit's accomplice rips the bag off her head.

I stop dead. A Klingons bumps into me. "Sorry, sorry," I say, staring in disbelief at the second figure from my past to pop up today.

Penelope!

I never wanted to see *her* again, even less than I wanted to see Finian.

Penelope Adele Saltzman was our stacker on the *Skint Idjit*. Every spaceship needs a stacker to handle the tricky bits, such as AI subroutine programming, which are beyond the intellectual capacity of ordinary human beings like you and me. Penelope was a donor, meaning she invested in the *Idjit* and donated her brainpower to our expeditions for non-mercenary reasons. Chiefly because she was in love with Donal.

Now she's standing on the gravsled, proclaiming, "This is a perfect example of how our politics have been corrupted by subservience to Big Tech!"

Ah, yes. There was that, too.

She waves the bag that was over her head like a black flag. The party guests stare. They're all stackers like her, but they don't know her. She rejected this glittering lifestyle long ago. Then I almost killed her—by accident!—but she got safely back to civilization aboard the *Marauding Elephant,* which was Finian's ship before he went into law enforcement.

She points an accusing finger at Finian. "You! You used to fight the establishment. Now you *are* the establishment."

"Amn't," Finian says, weakly. He's as gobsmacked as myself. Thank God I've got my beak on, and I'm at a safe distance. "What are you doing here?"

"I'm with him, obviously," says Penelope, nodding at Increpit. The notorious claim-jumper sits at her feet, gazing up at her adoringly, holding the end of the chains that are still wrapped around her wrists and neck. I swallow a nervous laugh, remembering that she was into BDSM, as well as activism. She's finally found someone who understands her needs. "We co-authored the one-man play about the Silicon People you heard earlier," she explains.

Some guests start to shout out how brilliant the play was. Clearly it all makes sense to them now: a lowlife like Increpit could never have written that, but a stacker like Penelope could have.

"The very fact that we won first place," Penelope announces, "proves that all of you are mentally enslaved to alien civilizations!"

Hang on, I thought it was the establishment we were all enslaved to?

Penelope rattles her chains. "Humanity has become a slave race! We don't think for ourselves anymore! We don't dream for ourselves anymore! All we do is pick up the trash left behind by dead aliens. And what's worse, the exploration industry has fallen completely under the sway of Big Tech and Wall Street. It's *their* money that funds exploration, *their* agendas that drive the search for A-tech, and *their* desires that shape our engagement with the galactic civilizations of the past! No one can make a living anymore without mortgaging their souls to the industrial-financial-technological complex!"

She's got a point there, actually.

"It's performance art," says a Klingons to a Sagittarian near me.

The Sagittarian nods. "I'm just like, yes. THIS."

Relaxing, I move on as Penelope continues to lecture the guests about what tools they are. It's just performance art. Where the feck is Sam? This is our chance to make our getaway, while Finian's stuck in the middle of the crowd. Penelope has incorporated him into her piece as a living example of an independent 'explorer' who was forced to knuckle under to the establishment.

There's Sam, coming out of the elevator, his bowtie undone, his hair mussed. Over here, Sam!

But I daren't wave to him. And now the idjit is slowing down to stare at the amazing sight of Penelope, in chains, calling King Zuckerberg's guests filthy elitists, and them lapping it up and livestreaming the whole thing on their smartphones.

I'm about to go and drag Sam away from the spectacle when the Krells overtake me. They've all got their rubber heads back on, and they're heading for the parking area. Looks like they plan to leave early, too.

"Taxi!" shouts one of them. "Taxi!"

Oh no, you don't! I break into a run. Squeezing through a gap between two private cars, which the Krells cannot fit through on account of their tails, I fall into the front seat of our taxi. "Go, go, go!" I gasp.

"But Sam," Imogen says, craning over the steering wheel.

"Leave him! He'll be all right! Just go!"

"Is that really Finian?"

"It is," I say in exasperation. "And he hasn't spotted us, but he might at any moment, so just *go,* you stupid cow!"

I am not very nice to Imogen, am I?

But Christ, if you knew her history of bailing when the grass looks greener elsewhere. She can't be trusted. I was all for leaving her out of this operation. It was Donal and Harriet who took pity on her, saying she'd shared our trials on the Lost Planet and deserved a second chance. Also, she *is* a good driver.

She reacts to my rudeness only by wrinkling her pretty nose. "Have you got the Gizmo?"

"Yes! I've got it!"

"Oh," she says. "I thought Sam did," and she puts the taxi in gear.

"Taxi! TAXI!" shout the Krells.

Imogen leans out the driver's side window. "Sorry! I've already got a passenger."

We are parked in, but that's not a problem for a vehicle equipped with anti-grav.

The taxi starts to rise into the air.

Not fast enough.

The Krells surround the taxi, wrench open the rear doors, and tumble in one after the other.

These taxis are not what you may be picturing. They aren't

your ordinary flying cars. They're nuclear-powered mini-spaceships, capable of getting into orbit and back. The pressurizable, airlock-equipped cabin is on the front. It's the two front seats and a large passenger compartment with seats along the sides. So there's more than enough room in the back for six people dressed in Krell suits that make them look like skinny toads with the tails of diplodocuses.

Sam jumps on the roof of a Maserati, makes a flying leap, and grabs my door, which I'm holding open for him. Red-faced and panting, he scrambles over my lap. "Hey, who are these bozos?"

I slam my door. The taxi is now a good ten feet up. Faces are starting to turn our way. We can't throw the Krells out. It would take too long and attract too much attention. "Feck it. We'll have to just take them. We'll drop them off at the spaceport on the moon. Go, go!"

"Fasten your seatbelts," Imogen yells.

The taxi rises another twenty feet into the air and banks to the left.

"To get out of these domes," Imogen says, "you have to get up to 160 kph. It's really stupid, actually."

"What's that in miles?" I say tensely. She is Canadian. Ireland went back to the imperial system after leaving the EU.

"I dunno. About a hundred miles an hour?"

Faster than that, I would say, based on the way we're accelerating. We scream around the inside of the bubble, over people's heads.

"It's gonna be like freaking Formula One in here when everyone tries to leave," Imogen says with relish. "Hey, Krells! Have you got your seatbelts on?"

Of course they haven't. No seatbelt would close around those costumes, so instead they're wriggling out of the costumes. There's the woman I tried to kiss at dinner. She's Chinese or something like that. All of them are, actually.

"I'm sealing the cabin," Imogen shrieks. She stamps on the accelerator, and we zoom out of the bubble-terminal, into the stratosphere. The canopy of King Zuck's tree shrinks to a dark green blob.

I exhale in relief, and pull off my beak.

Sam makes a queer choking noise. I twist around.

One of the former Krells is twisting the ends of Sam's bowtie around his throat like a garotte.

My little friend from the party crawls between my seat and Imogen's. A gun appears in her hand. This is not the non-lethal type of gun they sell for self-defense. It's the real deal, the type that shoots bullets that put holes in you and make you bleed and maybe die.

"Take us to the moon," she says, pointing the gun with rock-steady aim at Imogen's head.

CHAPTER 3

"You're in luck," I say smoothly to the Chinese woman pointing a gun at Imogen's head. "We were going to the moon, anyway."

Imogen has frozen up. Her hands grip the wheel, white-knuckled. We're no longer gaining altitude, but drifting.

My brain has frozen up, too, but my mouth is still going. This often happens at times of great stress. It gives people the impression that nothing terrifies me, which couldn't be further from the truth.

"Put the gun away, darlin'," I say, "unless you fancy a mid-air collision? No, I didn't think so."

The upper atmosphere twinkles with the headlights of cars and other taxis. Even on Treetop, where everyone flies everywhere, you don't usually see this much traffic heading into orbit. Of course, it's because of the Ghost Train. I'd completely forgotten about that. People are travelling into low orbit to see it up close. Idjits. It'll be here for another 25 hours.

But the traffic gives us cover for our getaway. The

Chinese woman moves the gun out of Imogen's field of vision. Her compatriot stops strangling Sam. I promise with fervent sincerity, on Sam's behalf and my own, that we'll not try anything. We all sit in stiff silence as Imogen, handling the controls with robotic care, takes us into a polar orbit at 13,000 miles up, and peels out into deep space. Destination: Arnold.

Yes, Treetop's moon has a name. It is Arnold. I think it was the name of the discoverer's dog or something. Everyone just calls it 'the moon' except when they need to distinguish it from Earth's moon.

I say into the silence, "It is Arnold you're wanting to go to, right? Not our moon? Because these taxis don't go *that* far." Treetop is 700 lightyears from Earth. "Ha, ha."

After a minute of excruciating silence, the woman says, "Yes. We're going to Arnold."

She's kneeling on the floor, covering Imogen with her gun. The others are sitting on the seats, checking their phones and chatting in Chinese. I'm fairly sure the fella right behind me has a gun, too, hidden under the deflated Krell tail he's draped over his lap. He's still got the rest of his Krell costume on. The head watches me with glittering orange eyes, animatronic tongue flickering over froggy lips.

Apart from that, the scene is so ordinary, it's surreal. I'm twisted sideways in my seat, elbow on the seatback, chatting.

"Your name was May, right?"

While I wait for the gunslinger to decide if she'll answer me, my gaze wanders to Sam, slumped in a corner seat, rubbing his throat. I hope to God he's not going to do anything stupid. He's got violent crime in his DNA. His mother styled herself the empress of the Omega Centauri cluster until Finian caught up with her.

"Maude. Anyway, that isn't my real name," the gunslinger responds, after so long I'd forgotten my question.

"Right, right. I'm rubbish with names. So what's on the moon, Maude? A sales convention?"

Sam speaks up. "They're from the XS Group," he says hoarsely. "I saw that dude's tattoo when he grabbed me." His lips tremble with emotion, as if he might spit at our hijackers.

"What's the XS Group?" I say.

"Jeez. The Extreme Sales Group. I've heard of them, and I'm not even from Earth."

Oh. I have heard of them, too.

I had a sort of a feeling, to be honest, when they took off their Krell suits and I saw all those Chinese faces. Even in our brave new interstellar age, when the opening of the galaxy has supposedly united all the nations in a mad headlong rush for loot, people tend to stick together with others like themselves. And that is doubly true when they're up to no good. It was certainly true of us in the old days. A third of the late, lamented *Skint Idjit's* crew hailed from County Clare, and we were on the fiddle if you like, cheating our backers out of every penny we could pocket.

But we didn't harass, stalk, and threaten people with guns.

That is the least of what the Extreme Sales Group gets up to, according to the internet. They're a Hong Kong-based outfit that hires out salespeople like mercenaries. If your product is dying on its feet, hire an XS salesperson and they'll make it sell. Guaranteed.

I always wondered why they don't leave a trail of lawsuits in their wake, and now I know. Dead men tell no tales …

and bring no lawsuits.

I'm not surprised their MO includes hasty exits from high-end parties. But why us? We were in the wrong place at the wrong time, that's all. The damnable luck of the Irish strikes again.

My moment of self-pity ends abruptly when Maude, not her real name, orders me to place my hands in full view. She elbows between the front seats and checks the radar and lidar readouts, changes the settings, checks again. Lastly she turns on the shortwave radio and listens to several minutes of traffic reports. The gun's hovering in my peripheral vision, and Maude is so close I can smell her shampoo. She really had me fooled. Then again, I'm easily fooled. Just ask Imogen.

Finally satisfied, Maude retreats to her place on the floor in the back. She leaves the radio blathering about heavy traffic in Treetop orbit and don't get too close to the Ghost Train. "OK. We aren't being pursued. That's good for us." She frowns thoughtfully. "Maybe not so good for you."

"Sure why would anyone be chasing us?" I say, all innocent, sweating like a pig.

"Oh, maybe because this mental defective," she gestures at the fella with his Krell costumes still on, "smashed a display case in King Zuck's private museum, and stole an A-tech artefact worth millions of dollars?"

The guy convulsively clutches his Krell tail. It's not a gun hidden under there. It's whatever he stole.

The light of acquisitiveness ignites in Sam's eyes. He leans forward. "What'd you grab, buddy?"

The question excites all the Krells. They jabber in Chinese. Maude does not join in. She just sits there grinding her teeth.

The one with dyed blond hair continues checking his phone. He's the one who choked Sam. I can see the edge of the tattoo Sam referred to poking out of his sleeve. Watching them, I'm revising my assumptions. Only those two are armed. If I could deal with them ... But I'm not starting anything on board a small craft in deep space. Been there, done that, got the blood all over me.

The thief lifts the edge of his costume to reveal—

—a tangle of wires and cloudy crystals.

These A-tech artefacts always look so unimpressive when you see them for yourself. Just like the Gizmo. But if Maude says that's worth millions, I believe her. The Gizmo, after all, is worth *billions,* and that reminds me, where is it? I feel inside my paunch, the back of the seat concealing my movements from the hijackers.

The thief struggles with English. The lips of his costume head move in sync with his words. "This," he says, "makes us swim underwater. We are amphibian! This is our culture. Live on land, hunt in water! This crystal substance absorbs oxygen from water, gives us air! It was in Zuckerberg museum, but it is *ours.*" He's cradling the ancient Krell artefact like a teddy-bear, smiling gleefully.

"So you just took it!" Sam says. "Way to go!" He winks at me. I shoot him an unguarded grin, understanding immediately. The alarm that summoned Finian and his merry men must have been set off by the Krells! The timing fits. That's why they were in such a hurry to leave. *We've* got away scot-free!

Apart from them being in our taxi, of course.

And the Gizmo not coming to hand, no matter how much I feel around inside my pouch.

"Look," the thief says. "We wear it like this!" He starts fitting the stolen artefact over his Krell head. A piece of wire falls off.

Imogen pipes up, her voice shaky. "Oh, I get it! You guys are biomodders."

I halt my search for the Gizmo, startled. She's right.

The thief is not wearing an animatronic Krell head. It's *his* head. It's joined to his thin pale neck.

'Biomod,' of course, is short for biomodification. That's tech-speak for cosmetic surgery that makes you look like an alien. I can't be bothered with the jargon, personally; I just call them nutters. But there is no denying that that is one of the finest biomods I've ever seen.

"He's the Chinese national champion of biomodification, Krell division," Maude says. Each word sounds like she's biting on something bitter. "The others are also Krells. Pre-surgery. You saw the costumes. So they got invited to this party. And what do the fucking morons do but smash the place up, set off the burglar alarms, and grab this thing they think is *theirs?*"

"Yowch," Imogen says sympathetically. "Are you going to be in trouble with your boss?"

The biomodification world is notably shady. I didn't know there was such a thing as the Chinese national championships, but I'm not surprised that the champions have minders like this. After all, the money for their surgeries has to come from somewhere.

"If they get arrested?" Maude says. "I'm going to be in trouble like you can't even imagine."

"Oh, I can imagine," Imogen says. "I work for the Bratva."

The Bratva—the Brotherhood—are the Russian mob who run Arcadia. See what I mean about arseholes sticking together? This is actually a Bratva taxi. If it were to vanish, and us with it, the Bratva would miss the taxi; they wouldn't miss Imogen. But I see what she's doing. She's trying to impress Maude by letting on that we are connected.

Right now I've got other things on my mind. I feel around inside my paunch with increasing panic. Where is the bloody Gizmo? Could I have dropped it? I definitely had it when I got into the taxi. It must have fallen on the floor.

My size 13 duck-toed Denebite boots rest on a solid layer of fast food wrappers, coffee cups, dead electronics, batteries, sweaters and scarves, and various other items left behind by passengers, which are *supposedly* being stored with care until their owners collect them. I'd have to get down on the floor and do a proper search, and I can't do that with Maude on guard, her gaze roving back and forth between Imogen and me, her gun resting on her knee.

Is she planning to sit there for the next seven hours?

That's how long it takes to get to Treetop's moon in a taxi.

The answer is no, she's not. After half an hour she orders me out of the front seat. I have to sit in the back, in the opposite corner from Sam so we can't conspire. Maude takes my place beside Imogen. I alternate between terror that she'll look down and spot the Gizmo on the floor, even though I couldn't see it myself, and irritation that she and Imogen seem to be getting on so well. They start off chatting about security systems, and move on to fashion, music, and sexism in the world of organized crime. I get held up as an example, which is completely unfair. I'm not a criminal, organized or otherwise. I just …

… ended up here somehow.

I've plenty of time to contemplate all my mistakes, while the taxi chugs through space towards Arnold.

From Treetop, Arnold looks like it's made of blue cheese. Up close, it's more like Roquefort. The previous owners of Treetop—the Krells, as it happens—terraformed their moon in accordance with their fetish for giant vegetation, so each teal splotch is a gargantuan cactus. It's spectacular at ground level. So they say. I've never been here before. I don't give a feck, anyway. I peer eagerly at the viewscreen that hinges down from the taxi's ceiling, trying to spot the spaceport.

You can't land anything larger than a small passenger shuttle on the canopy of a Treetop tree. The leaves are strong but not *that* strong. Interstellar cargo ships can weigh in the hundreds of thousands of tons, and be up to half a mile long. I suppose they could have built a spaceport on the ground among the tree roots. But there was already an old Krell spaceport on the moon, so they just tidied that up, put in furniture suitable for humans, and carried on using it.

There it is, a gray blotch on the blue and beige surface. All of that isn't the spaceport, of course. It's warehouses and factories and long-term storage facilities and food processing plants and recycling centers—all the industrial shite that the residents of Treetop don't want on their lovely green planet. It sprawls out for hundreds of miles, literally visible from space.

And somewhere down there is our poor old ship, the *Intergalactic Bogtrotter*. Kenneth, Ruby, and Vanessa parked her there two months ago. They've been living on board, prepping the ship for her voyage to Pervée—that would be my rental planet (thanks, Russian programmers!). They must be going out of their minds at this point. We were meant to radio them after the heist and we haven't.

Maude yawns and stretches her arms over her head. "OK, I'll take over now."

"But," Imogen says.

"But nothing, bitch!" she screams. "MOVE!"

Zero to sixty on the rage-o-meter. Imogen scrambles out of the driver's seat. Maude takes her place.

We all sit in silence once more as Maude deorbits the taxi. Gee-force presses us back against our seats. The viewscreen fills with flames. Extreme aerobraking is the spaceship equivalent of drifting. Maude's risking all our lives to show us how upset she is.

The ground rushes up at us. Blue hills sprout forests of spikes. We swoop down over the giant cacti and hit the ground—not even a runway, but the bare desert. This madwoman has missed the spaceport altogether!

The taxi bumps to a halt, and we unbuckle. From the relaxed demeanor of the Krells, I gather this is where they expected to be.

"Out!" Maude puts on a pair of mirrored sunglasses and opens the driver's door. There's a gentle *whoomp* of escaping atmosphere.

It's like opening an oven … and climbing in.

Arnold's air is thin, the sky dark indigo. Even the Krells—the real ones—could not persuade a moon with less than 30% of Earth's gravity to hold onto a proper atmosphere. We've been acclimatizing all the way from Treetop, but all the same, I'm gasping. The air feels too thin and hot to breathe.

The Krells put on oxygen masks.

"Thanks for the ride," Maude says through her mask. "It was a big help." She points her gun at Imogen. "Step away from the taxi."

Imogen's picking flakes of carbon off the taxi's nose cone, which is a charred mess. That descent burnt off several inches of insulation. "You've wrecked my taxi," she says in a trembling voice.

"I said step away from the fucking vehicle!"

Imogen cringes and scuttles back. Poor girl. She thought she'd built up a rapport with Maude, and now she's confused.

Not me. I've met people like Maude before. The way she screamed at Imogen gave her away. She's annoyed, frustrated, and frightened by the way everything's gone so wrong, so she's going to take it out on us, because that's what sociopaths do.

Besides, it wouldn't do for anyone to find out they hijacked our taxi.

I bend over, as if trying to breathe better. I've still got the bottom half of my Denebite costume on. It's falling down around my hips. On the pretext of holding it up, I slide my right hand into my waistband.

CHAPTER 4

"Fucking move already!" Maude yells. "It's too hot to stand around out here!"

I straighten up, heart thudding. She's not about to shoot us, after all. She's trying to herd us away somewhere. I don't like that much, either.

Nor do I want to move away from the taxi, because it's got the Gizmo in it.

But Maude points her gun at me, and I decide obedience is the better part of valor. I give Imogen what I hope is an encouraging smile. "Cheer up, it's going to be fine," I whisper, and we follow the Krells.

Blondie walks ahead, talking on his phone. We all bounce awkwardly in the low gravity, except for Maude, who brings up the rear. She's got the loping micro-gravity gait dialed in, and her gun stays in her hand.

Heat ripples off the ground. It's as dry as a bone. The dust makes me cough. I lace my fingers over my eyes and squint through them. The rectangular outline of a building shimmers in the distance.

A flatbed lorry purrs past us, going in the other direction.

Walking sideways, I watch it shrink into a tarry blob and converge on the other blob which is Imogen's taxi. The whine of hydraulics cuts through the silence. They're loading the taxi onto the flatbed, taking it away.

"My taxi!" Imogen says.

My Gizmo! I think, stricken.

There it goes, gliding away into the haze. We have no option but to stumble on, into the shadow of the building. It's an industrial facility about a mile long. This side is lined with loading docks. Here and there, semi-trailers nuzzle their rear ends against the wall. They all have Chinese writing on their sides.

Maude herds us up a flight of concrete stairs and in through the side door of an unused loading dock.

Air-conditioning comes as a huge relief. It does not compensate for the smell, which is horrendous. So is the noise—clanking, whining, thudding, crunching.

We climb onto a tongue of rusty steel that sticks out over a conveyor belt as wide as a highway. The conveyor belt runs the entire length of the building, carrying rubbish towards a crusher apparatus at the far end.

It's a recycling center.

The rubbish inching past below includes kitchen waste, broken furniture, debris from Krell buildings (they're still demolishing shite to make room for more human facilities), and huge chunks of cactus, oozing goo from their fibrous ends.

"Hey, isn't this a recycling center?" Sam says, his voice too high.

"Yes," snaps Maude.

"But what about separating the trash? They're fanatical

about that on Treetop! Kitchen waste, cardboard, plastics, metal, it's all supposed to be recycled separately!"

Blondie looks up from his phone and speaks for the first time. His English is as fluent as Maude's. "Oh, that's just PR bullshit. It makes them feel good. But it all goes into the same incinerator. Now we've got a whole galaxy to pollute, who cares?"

"And the incinerator runs hot," Maude says with a dark chuckle. "No one can tell from the ashes *what* went in there, whether it's plastics … or cactuses … or human remains."

She raises her gun, sights on the thief, and shoots him in the heart. Then she shoots the other former Krells. *Pop, pop, pop.*

It all happens in a few seconds flat. While we're still staring, too stunned to react, she goes back and puts another bullet into the head of each writhing body.

Blondie says consolingly to us, "It's just business."

I find my voice. "How is it just business?"

"They screwed up."

Maude rolls the bodies off the side. They fall ten feet to the conveyor belt, and are carried slowly away.

"Damn," she says. "Out of ammo. Can you handle the rest?"

"Sure thing," Blondie says. He raises his gun and sights on Imogen, who backs away towards the end of the platform. Her hair's coming out of its bun, falling down over the collar of her taxi driver's uniform. Terror bleaches her face.

Maude's patting her pockets in annoyance, searching for her spare clip, I suppose. That gives me the moment I need to reach into the waistband of my Denebite costume and pull out my lightsaber.

Here are the mistakes Maude and Blondie made:

1. They didn't make me take off the bottom half of my costume.
2. They assumed I was a harmless party guest. (I assumed the same thing about them, of course, until disillusioned.)
3. They picked Imogen to murder first.

Imogen has made it fairly clear to me in the past that going through a garbage compactor would be too good for me. To be honest, I feel the same way about her sometimes. But letting this happen to her is not an option.

I switch my lightsaber on and stab Blondie in the back. Piercing guilt paralyzes me for a second as he goes down as if struck by an axe. Maude's mouth falls into an O of astonishment. Her hand drops to her gun—which is empty, thank God.

Sam leaps at her with a despairing yell. They topple to the floor in a clinch, punching and kicking, and I can't use my lightsaber for fear of hitting Sam.

My lightsaber, if you're just joining us, is a fearsome weapon. I found it on the Draco spur twenty years ago when I was working for Finian. It looks like a slim baton with alien writing on it, with a powerpack that swings down like a stock, and it emits laser pulses so fast that they appear to blend into a solid beam. It's like the ones in Star Wars except better, because it's got an adjustable range of about thirty yards.

Blondie heaves himself onto one elbow. Pain twists his face into a grimace. There's smoke and steam coming out of the hole in his back! I must not have hit anything vital. Or else he's on some fearsome drugs. Actually, that would explain a lot. He reaches with a trembling hand for his gun, which he dropped when he went down.

Imogen reaches it first. Screaming wordlessly, she snatches up the gun and shoots Blondie in the face.

I'm busy trying to kick Maude away from Sam, so I only see it out of the corner of my eye. Blood splatters the platform.

Maude and Sam have rolled dangerously near the edge of the platform. Maude lands a karate chop on Sam's neck. Stunned, Sam loosens his stranglehold on her—

—and both of them go over the side, and fall to the conveyor belt.

Without even thinking about it, I leap down after them.

Sam howls, half-buried in a chunk of cactus. He landed in a sitting position as if the cactus were a deep sofa.

Maude's on her feet, running back along the conveyor belt, zigzagging around the piles of rubbish.

I chase her, holding the bottom half of my Denebite costume up with one hand, slashing my lightsaber wildly at her back. I don't want to hurt her, but I can't let her fetch reinforcements. I slice a pile of household garbage in half, and it cascades across the conveyor belt, blocking my way. I jump on top of it, and sink knee-deep into fruit rinds, coffee grounds, leftovers, and—judging by the smell—dog poop.

Feck! I haul my feet out of the reeking mess. Maude's so far ahead I can no longer see her. Anyway, what's the point of chasing her? She had her phone. She'll have called for back-up already.

I peel the bottom half of my Denebite costume off over my boots, wipe my hands on it, and throw it down. We've got to find transport and get out of here.

"Fletch! *Fletch!*"

Sam's voice is barely audible over the grinding noise of the compactor, but I can hear his panic.

I charge back the way I came. The conveyor belt has been moving all the time, so I'm only a few yards past where I started out. I glance up at the loading platform. I can't see Imogen anymore.

But I haven't got time to stop. Sam's cries are getting louder and more frantic. I dash along the conveyor belt towards the compactor.

There he is, still stuck in that fecking chunk of cactus!

He's struggling desperately to get out, but he obviously can't. A few yards beyond him, the packer blade of the compactor slams down on a pile of construction debris. It slowly pulverizes fiberboard and polysteel and Krell regocrete. Dust billows over us.

I grab Sam's hands and pull. All that happens is I lose my footing and end up in his lap. The problem is the micro-gravity.

Another problem is he's covered in cactus juice. On my next effort, our hands slide apart as if covered with grease.

"Why are you stuck?" I scream.

"Because this shit is very fucking sticky!" he screams back.

The compactor swallows the construction debris. As the packer blade rises again, heat blasts my face. A sullen orange glow radiates from beyond.

The blade descends on the other end of the piece of cactus Sam's stuck in, and sucks it under, inch by inch. Juice squirts all over us, stinging when it gets in my eyes.

I whip my lightsaber out of my pocket. "Tuck your legs and arms in!" I chop off the bit of cactus he's sitting in. It tumbles loose, pitching him onto his side.

The packer blade grinds down to the belt, inches from my feet. I skitter back. The blade rises again.

Sam crawls back along the conveyor belt on hands and knees, with a lump of cactus still stuck to his bottom.

The packer blade starts to fall.

I pick Sam up, cactus and all, and stagger with him across the conveyor belt. I throw him over the guard rail to the floor. Then I jump after him.

"Thank feck for micro-gravity!" I say breathlessly, picking myself up.

He's thanking me profusely for saving his life. Well may he. I suspect he *wouldn't* have done the same for me.

"Can you get that shite off you?"

We're in a concrete ditch under the loading platforms. If Maude and / or her reinforcements show up now, we'll be sitting ducks.

I flinch as a torrent of fabric cascades off the end of the nearest unloading platform, onto the conveyor belt. It looks like carpets.

Right. I climb up on the guard rail, grab the edge of the nearest descending carpet, and flip myself onto the platform above. I feel like a Olympic gymnast. Micro-gravity definitely has its points.

I land upright on the loading platform, staring into the face of a Chinese party in dungarees and a baseball cap, whose arms are full of carpets.

"Drop the carpet," I say, showing him my lightsaber. It looks a bit like a gun when I'm holding it by the powerpack.

His hands fly into the air.

"Good, now lie down on the floor! Hands behind your head!"

I'm getting good at this, amn't I?

And the better I get at it, the less I like myself.

"Sam, can you climb up the carpet?"

It's a *red* carpet, the kind of runner they use at celebrity events. Quite ironic. I flip and shake it until the end falls into the ditch where Sam is tearing bits of cactus off his bum. He clings to it and I haul him up.

"Brilliant. Now—" I address the fella on the floor. "Give us your car keys. D'you speak English? Car keys!"

"Don't you want my phone as well," he says into the floor, "so that I can't call management?"

"Good thinking, sir. Yes, I'll have the phone as well."

He hands both items over. "I'll testify against them if you like?" he offers.

"Aye well, that's your lookout. Testifying against the XS Group is not a wise move, as far as I know, but that's only based on films."

"Oh. I thought you were the police."

Sam laughs out loud at that.

"No," I say, "but thanks for the keys. We'll be seeing you."

"What's this fancy new NEPD *for?*" the lorry driver complains. "If they can't even crack down on fraudulent recycling practices …"

We leave him contemplating the uselessness of the NEPD. He's right—they *are* useless. But the more I think about it, the more I suspect they were designed that way. The politicians deliberately hamstrung them so they couldn't interfere too much with organized crime in the colonies.

The shutter door at the back of the platform has been rolled up and a semi-trailer half full of carpets is docked with it. We could walk straight in. "You go in the back," I tell Sam.

"Why?"

"You'll not be able to sit down with a cactus stuck to your arse, will you?"

I hurry through the side door, out into the daylight, and down the stairs. The shadow of the building has shrunk. It now slices across the parked lorries. "Imogen!" The silence rings in my ears. "Imogen!"

Oh, feck. I *knew* she was not to be trusted.

I run along the side of the building. I can't remember which of all these many doors we went in at.

My legs start to tremble as the adrenaline wears off. Muscle cramps shoot through my limbs. I'm not an Olympic gymnast, after all. Just an Irishman on the wrong side of the law and the wrong side of history.

"Imogen! IMOGEN!"

"Fletch!"

To my extreme relief, Imogen's voice carries over the desert. She comes running through the sunlight, a blurry streak.

"This way!" I windmill my arms.

She must have given up on us and set out by herself, hoping to make it across the desert on foot. She's come back because she thinks her chances are better with me. I hope she's right.

I bang on the side and hear an answering bang. "Is that Sam?" Imogen says.

"Yeah. He's in the back."

She squints at me for a long second, then nods. "I don't trust him, either."

"It's not that," I say, although it is. Partly, it is. He wasn't part of the old crew and he's not from Ireland. We may have worked together to plan this heist, but when you come right down to it, ours is a partnership of convenience, which began with us trying to kill one another.

And that actually goes for Imogen, too. So I don't open up that can of worms. I just tell her about the sticky cactus, which makes her laugh.

We climb into the cab and I stick the key in the ignition.

"I've never driven a lorry before," I say. "Hope I don't crash it into anything."

Ha, ha. There is nothing to crash into. The desert stretches as empty as a snooker table with no balls on it. All quiet for now, but how long will it stay that way? I keep expecting Maude to burst out of the recycling center with guns blazing.

"Where did you get the keys?" Imogen feels her cheeks. "Ow. I'm sunburned."

"I took them off a fella delivering carpets."

Thankfully the lorry's an automatic. I put it in gear. For a minute nothing happens. Then a squealing, clashing noise comes from behind us, and the lorry leaps forward. I think I just pulled the loading door out of the wall.

"I can drive," Imogen says.

"No, I need you to navigate." I hand her the lorry driver's phone.

Imogen regards the phone with distaste. Fair enough, it's got pornographic decals around the screen. Then she looks across at me and utters the words I've been dreading.

"You've still got the Gizmo, haven't you?"

"No. I left it in the taxi." I forestall her cry of despair. "But we're going to get it back."

I accelerate. The lorry gathers speed, bouncing across the desert, and takes off ungracefully into the air.

CHAPTER 5

"Do you actually *know*," Imogen says, biting off her words, which makes her sound like Maude, "where the taxi *is?*"

"It got towed," I remind her. "I assume Maude wanted to get rid of it fast. So it'll be in the local impound lot. Could you check on the phone and find out where that is?"

Like any modern vehicle, the lorry has stubby wings. These are only for balance, not for lift. The antigrav does the hard work. I fly low over the desert. Glancing down at our shadow, I can see that a number of carpets are flapping out the back. Good thing no one's around to see.

Imogen looks up from the lorry driver's phone. "Guess how many tow lots there are on Arnold?"

"A lot?"

"Fifteen. There must be a lot of bad drivers on this moon." She sighs. I know the carnage in the recycling center affected her. She's trying not to break down, and succeeding, mostly. "Anyway, I've got the GPS working, so now we know where we are. It's like a hundred klicks to the spaceport. I guess we should try the nearest tow lot first." She sticks the phone in my face. It's all in Chinese.

"It's all in Chinese," I say. "That's very helpful."

"It is," she says, not picking up on my sarcasm. She never does.

"Can you *read* that?"

"Yeah, I took Chinese in college."

"Next you'll be telling me that by the way, you also play the ukulele."

"I do."

"Ah, come on."

She laughs out loud. "Just kidding. All I can play is the kazoo." She investigates the glove compartment. "Oh look, Fletch, green tea. Hydrate."

"Thanks." I swig the revolting stuff while wrestling with the steering. Keeping a twenty-tonner straight in the air is no joke. I should have let Imogen drive, but then I'd be stuck trying to decipher the GPS in Chinese.

"Left up here," she says.

"At the cactus?"

"Yep."

We swerve around the base of a cactus the size of Mullaghmore. It's shaped like a knobbly, bulgy, blue-green pincushion. Scabby brown sabres, up to thirty feet long, stick out of it at all angles. Imagine pricking your finger on one of those. There are rags caught on them, which lift off in black flurries as we approach. Birds. They whirl away from the lorry, shrieking so loudly we can hear them even with the windows closed and the A/C on.

"It's about thirty kilometers," Imogen says.

"What's that in miles?"

She smiles and aims a mock swat at my head.

Mission accomplished: I've cheered her up. She isn't going

to fall apart on me. What's next? Right.

"We need to get in touch with Kenneth, Vanessa, and Ruby. Ring them and tell them we're on our way, but we'll be slightly delayed."

"OK. I'll try calling Van." She gets out her own phone—which doesn't work here, of course, as we both use Arcadia-based carriers—and copies the number onto the lorry driver's phone.

"Don't mention that we've temporarily mislaid the Gizmo," I say uneasily. "No need to worry them."

"All right."

Ring, ring.

"She's not picking up."

"It's an unknown number; she's being careful. Try leaving a message."

"Hey, Van, this is Imogen. Call me."

She repeats the process twice more. Kenneth and Ruby aren't picking up, either.

"Okayyyy," Imogen whispers. She's got her knuckles in her mouth. "Let's act like this is *not* a very bad sign. Let's just pretend they all went out for pizza and forgot their phones."

As calmly as I can manage, I say, "They'll probably call back in a minute. Which way up here?"

We're zooming between two mountainous cacti, along a dry valley lined with thorns. The sun's in our faces now, so the windscreen has tinted itself dark, turning everything sepia.

"Turn right after this cactus," Imogen mutters, pinching and swiping the phone's screen.

The valley opens out. I slew the lorry to the right. Now, instead of bare desert below, we're skimming over Krell architecture. The Krell were aliens with exceedingly strange mindsets. We call them Krell because they had tails, and *may* have been amphibious, but beyond that we know nothing about them. Their terraformed planets only add to the mystery. They liked grossly oversized vegetation but they also liked cramped, labyrinthine cities. The built-up area below resembles one of those mazes you get in children's coloring books, and it goes on forever. Nothing moves down there.

The sun throws the shadow of the lorry onto the cactus slope on our right. We have an entourage of smaller, raggedy shadows. They're flocking around the back.

"It's those birds!"

"I hope Sam is OK back there," Imogen says.

I have already come to the conclusion that he may not be OK, and am looking for somewhere to land. The streets of the Krell maze are too narrow for the lorry. There is nowhere except the slope of the cactus. Right. Down we go. Our right wing clips a spike, the lorry spins, and I get her wheels down with her nose pointing uphill.

"Next time, let me drive," Imogen says.

"With pleasure." I jump out. Birds rise up like scraps of burnt paper from the lorry, and I run around the back, dreading what I may find.

A roll of carpet tumbles out and unrolls itself on the slope at my feet. Sam sits up, eyes on top of his head. "Are they gone?"

"The birds? Up there. What happened to your trousers?"

He's only wearing his boxer shorts and the shirt from his tuxedo. The tails flap around his skinny legs. "That cactus shit was not coming off. Jeez, we're *on* a cactus!"

It's springy underfoot. In combination with the micro-gravity it feels like walking on a trampoline.

"Were the birds attacking you or what were they doing?"

They're starting to come back. A bold one flaps straight into the back of the lorry.

"Oh man," Sam says. "You know what's in there? Bodies."

"What?!?" Imogen and I say at nearly the same time.

"Yup. Corpses. When the carpets, like, fell out the back, it uncovered a whole pile of them. I guess those assholes make a practice of recycling human remains. As they demonstrated when they whacked the Krell."

I start towards the back of the lorry.

"No, Fletch, you do *not* want to see them ..."

But I have to. I vault into the back of the lorry. It's now empty but for a couple of birds standing on ...

I suppose they were bodies, before a flock of alien vulture-analogs dined on them.

Now, they've got no faces. Entrails spill from ragged cavities. There were two of them.

I just saw four people murdered in front of my face half an hour ago, but this is worse, somehow.

I gag, and jump back down, ducking to avoid another half-dozen birds which are flapping in to rejoin their lunch companions at the buffet.

"Where do you figure they came from?" Sam says. If he's queasy, it doesn't show. His eyes are bright.

"I don't know and I don't care." I start to walk away from the lorry. Then I go back for the useful stuff out of the cab: the half-gallon bottle of green tea, mostly full, and the driver's sunglasses. Then I start walking again. The sunglasses help. They hide my eyes, and the tears that are threatening to fall. Jesus but that was a horrible sight.

After a minute, Imogen and Sam catch up with me.

"Where are you going?" Sam says.

"I'm not driving a lorry with that in the back."

Imogen does not argue, from which I gather she had a peek for herself. She says, "Well, we can walk to the tow lot. It's only a couple more kilometers."

Then we have to fill Sam in about the reason we are going to the tow lot in the first place.

There are some expostulations, I am sorry to say, and not all of them come from Sam. It's hot, we're all tired, the thin air is making our heads ache, and the silence of Arnold is somehow horrible. Even our own arguing voices are a better sound.

After the futile discussion dies down, Imogen rekindles conversation with, "I know where they came from, anyway."

She means the bodies.

"Does it say on there?" I ask.

She's holding the lorry driver's phone, tilting it and squinting to see the screen in the sunlight.

"Kind of, yeah. See this? OK, it's in Chinese, sorry. This is a map of where the driver went today. So this was his only stop before the recycling center. And this says, I don't actually know this character, but the others say something like 'New You Reform Clinic."

"Organ harvesting?" Sam says. "My mom dabbled in that for a while …"

"They can print replacement organs now," I tell him, suppressing my disgust. He comes from Omega Centauri, so you can never be quite sure what he knows. I'd like to think that explains his lack of morals, too.

"Well, yeah, I was about to say, she dabbled in it for a while, and then printable organs got big and knocked the bottom out of the market."

"Was that when you lived in the Omega Centauri cluster?"

"Nope, before that, when we lived on Cygnus 2c. There were always explorers coming through, so supply wasn't a problem."

And you wonder why I do not trust Sam? He grew up thousands of lightyears from Earth—he's never even been to Earth—with a mother who's got more blood on her hands than Genghis Khan. *Slight* exaggeration.

"So as I was saying," Imogen begins, and the lorry blows up.

I hear the whistling screech, and by the time the boom comes, I'm flat on my face with Imogen underneath me.

I twist my upper body, keeping her pinned— "That was a fecking *rocket!*"

The lorry is a blackened, windowless hulk. Flames boil from the engine compartment. That's the big drawback of hydrogen fuel cells. Smoke rises towards the wispy contrail the rocket left in the sky

Imogen pushes at my chest. "Let me up," she says, and I do.

Sam's dancing and yelling, thinking he saw where the rocket came from. Somewhere over that way—meaning the maze city that stretches to the horizon. That narrows it down all right.

"Throw away the phone," I tell Imogen.

"Why?" Pale, she cuddles it obstinately to her chest.

"Throw away the fecking phone!"

There is a short tussle, which ends with me holding the

phone and Imogen crying. I hurl it as far as I can. With a micro-gravity assist, it ends up in the nearest street of the maze city.

Five seconds later, another rocket hurtles out of the sky and blows the street up.

CHAPTER 6

Debris from the explosion in the maze city patters down around us. The largest pieces tear divots out of the cactus.

We run. It's more of a panicked sprint than a rational retreat. After all, we have no more working electronics on us that could be targeted. But when you don't know who's shooting at you, or from where, every passing second comes loaded with fear, and the sky itself turns into an enemy.

But you can't run away from the sky. When we get out of breath we straggle to a halt.

We've been running around the cactus hill, parallel to its knobbly crown. We stand on one of the knolls that the spikes sprout out of, gazing down at a sea of destruction.

This part of the maze city has been razed. This is what we humans call colonizing the galaxy. It's done with bulldozers.

A few months or years from now, there will be factories, feedlots, fuel depots, and God knows, probably an outlet mall here.

At the moment there's only an expanse of rubble. Down at the base of the cactus, a wire box fence surrounds an impound lot.

Or rather, a scrap yard. On one side of the long, rectangular lot, vehicles are stacked on top of each other, two and three deep. On the other side, shinier vehicles stand at random angles—soon to be scrap, as well, when they've been stripped of resalable components. Well, that's one way to get rid of an inconvenient taxi.

From here, I can see several winged blobs that *might* be it. Or might not. We'll just have to go and see.

Sam points. "There's a kiosk at the gate. See? There will be guards. I want some kind of a weapon."

"I've got my lightsaber."

"But *I* haven't got a weapon. They took my .22 *and* my pocket taser."

I think to myself that this is a good thing. "Imogen?"

She's sitting on the knoll. Our desperate sprint has worn her out. Her head hangs. I pass her the green tea, and she finishes it. Neither Sam nor I say a word.

At last she pushes herself to her feet. "OK, I'm as ready as I'll ever be."

We walk downhill.

The kiosk, at the far end of the lot, is a trailer with small tinted windows. No one comes out to stop me from cutting a hole in the chainlink fence with my lightsaber. Maybe the place is unmanned, after all. Maybe the security guards are sat in the trailer watching the Ghost Train on television.

We walk among the undamaged vehicles on the right-hand side of the lot. It's so quiet I can hear the blood rushing through my ears. The wire roof overhead divides the sky into hexagons. There's a foul smell like rubbish decaying. These new arrivals are mostly cars, and they're mostly expensive sport and luxury models, and I'll bet their owners don't know where they are.

A few small spaceships loom over them. That one's not our taxi. Nor is that one, or that one …

"Oh my God," Imogen says. "There it is!"

She breaks into a run.

A lithe four-legged shape squirts out from under the stacked vehicles on the other side of the lot. It bounds after her.

Yelling, I run in pursuit. The blue lance of my lightsaber bites the ground at the creature's heels. It looks like a dog but it isn't.

Imogen looks back, sees the danger, screams. She leaps at the side of our taxi and fumbles with the passenger door.

The creature launches itself towards her—

—and my lightsaber gores it through the body. It collides harmlessly with the door of the taxi as Imogen dives in.

I catch up, and stab it again for good measure. It's a robot dog.

They used to use these in the exploration industry before immune boosters were discovered. In those days, every alien bacteria and organism could potentially kill you. So the early explorers EVA'd in spacesuits, and they used these robot dogs to investigate the planets where they landed.

Nowadays we all get A-tech immune shots, which are fecking miraculous. So I'm breathing in alien germs without ill effect, and there's no more call for robot dogs in the exploration industry—human labor is cheaper, when you take production costs into account. So this one's apparently been redeployed as a junkyard dog, because you do want security for your illegal auto stripping operation. It just isn't the kind of security I was expecting.

I lean against the side of our taxi, panting. The robot dog lies motionless at my feet. It's got a cluster of sensors instead of a head. Horrible-looking.

"Is it dead?" Imogen screams from inside the taxi.

"It was never alive," I say quietly, looking around for Sam. He's always wandering off.

Another robot dog pokes its sensor-blistered snout around the nearest car. I hold my lightsaber at the ready, watching the dog mince closer.

"Where did you leave the Gizmo, Fletch?"

"I don't know. Try looking under the seats."

"I can't see it!"

The second dog springs. I stab it in mid-air, feeling like a hunter of yore dispatching a wolf with my spear. I hope there aren't any more of them. Unlike a spear, my lightsaber does run out of charge, and I haven't got a spare … "Imogen, could you see if there's a spare powerpack in there?"

"I'm looking for the goddamn Gizmo!"

"It's in a resealable bag."

"I'm not seeing it!" Sounds of her scrabbling through the rubbish on the floor.

"It would help if your taxi wasn't a complete tip," I mutter.

Her feet vanish and her head pops out of the door. "Listen, asshole. While you were taking it easy on Arcadia, I was working twelve-hour shifts, ferrying rich stacker douchebags, oh so sorry, I'm repeating myself, all over the planet. I had to eat in the taxi, sleep in the taxi …"

"Taking it easy? Do you think working construction is *easy?*"

Even as I defend myself, I remember that working construction does have one side benefit: I'm fitter and stronger than I've ever been in my life. My hands are solid calluses and my upper body is solid muscle. Breaking up alien ruins all day builds up your stamina as well as your strength. So I'm probably much less tired than Imogen is, and I shouldn't be giving out to her.

"Sorry," I say.

After a few more minutes, she says in a small voice, "Got it."

"Good."

"Is this really it? It looks like a nail."

"That's it." I'm elated to have the Gizmo back. Honestly, I am. But Sam's still missing and another pair of robot dogs are watching me from behind the Porsche across the way. They'd be slavering if they had mouths.

Imogen kneels on the driver's seat of the taxi. "I found this, too." She holds up a McDonald's bag and two cans of Red Bull. "Bet you're glad now my taxi is such a tip ..."

The Mickey D's logo makes my mouth water. But instead of reaching for the bag, I take the Gizmo. This time it goes securely in the hip pocket of my jeans. I do all this onehanded, while watching the robot dogs.

"Now we just need to find Sam and get out of here," I say with false heartiness.

"Well, we're not going anywhere in this," Imogen says, slapping the taxi's steering-wheel. "The reactor's gone. So's the anti-grav engine."

"Bloody hell, that was fast."

"Bet you nothing else on this lot runs, either."

"And you didn't happen to find a spare powerpack in the

glove compartment, I suppose?"

"No."

"Feck."

A terrified shout peels me off the side of the taxi. An engine roars. I glance towards the gate, while keeping one eye on the robot dogs.

Gritty dust blows towards me. Two human figures run between the parked cars, arms pumping frantically. A bright red sports car looms out of the dust.

So *something* on this lot runs.

The red car accelerates, swerves at one of the runners, and catches him/her on its snarling grille. The person flies into the air like a broken doll. I take this all in before my heart's got time to skip a beat. The car mows down the other runner.

And then it accelerates straight at me.

I react without thinking. I grab Imogen around the waist and throw her onto the roof of the taxi like bloody Nijinsky. Thank you, micro-gravity! Then I step on the driver's seat and scramble up onto the roof.

The red car crunches into the driver's side of the taxi.

It wasn't actually going very fast at the moment of impact. All the same, the jolt knocks me and Imogen off the other side of the taxi.

I run back around, lightsaber in hand, mentally steeling myself to murder someone. I will if I have to. I will.

The red car backs a few feet away from the taxi. Its bumper is crumpled, its bonnet dented. It's a Lamborghini, if I know my hood ornaments. I can't see through the tinted windscreen.

The gull-wing driver's side door flies up, and Sam steps

out.

"Whoops," he says ruefully. "Sorry about that, man."

I stand there, thumb hovering over the press button of my lightsaber. I don't know what to do. Did he intend to run me down? Or was it really an accident?

He walks around the Lamborghini and makes a face at the damage. "I always wanted a car like this, and I have to wreck it."

Behind me, Imogen screams, "WATCH OUT!"

I then have to spend the next eternity, which actually lasts about ten seconds, dealing with the last two robot dogs.

Meanwhile, Sam jogs back towards the gate, shirttails flapping. To my shame, I had completely forgotten about the two people he mowed down. Maybe he's gone to see if they are all right ...

... or not. When he comes back, he is wearing an unfamiliar pair of trousers and a matching pair of sneakers.

"High five!" he grins through a mask of dust.

I leave his hand hanging in the air. As if robbing the dead wasn't enough, he may have attempted to kill me, too. I just don't know.

His face falls into a sulky pout. "Did you find the Gizmo?"

"Yeah. Who were those fellas? The security guards?"

"I assume, man, I assume," he shrugs. "I didn't check their ID. I walked into the kiosk and asked them if any of these cars run."

"That was risky. Did they raise the alarm?"

"No, man. Wimps. They told me the Lamborghini hasn't been stripped yet. Then they gave me the keys. I made them start the engine, just in case it would have blown up or something. Then I told them to run." Sam chuckles.

"You didn't even need a weapon."

A shadow passes across his expression. "Anything can be a weapon. That's what my mom always used to say."

Imogen's gone to examine the dead security guards. I jog over to her.

Squatting by Sam's second victim, she looks up at me speechlessly.

The security guard is an alien.

All right, all right. He / she is human. There are no aliens. They're all dead and we've inherited the galaxy.

But Jesus, this is a good copy of a Krell, if Krells were thin and tailless. The frog-mouthed face, the bald head with the frilly ears, the brown warty skin, same as the natterjack toads you find in Irish ponds… all the exposed skin, including hands and neck, matches. Dust films orange Krell eyes.

The other one's much the same.

I remember I was properly impressed by the so-called Chinese national champion of biomodding, Krell division. Silly me. He was just the product sample.

This one's much more realistic. And he (or maybe she) was working as a security guard at a scrap yard? That doesn't sound right.

Imogen stretches out a finger to touch a warty, dead cheek, and draws back swiftly. "Did I tell you what I found on the driver's phone? The New You Reform Clinic?"

"Do you think it's all connected?" I say sarcastically.

"God, you're such an idiot, Fletch! Of course it's all connected. It's a *biomodding* clinic. It has to be. And that character I couldn't read … I bet that's Chinese for Krell."

A few minutes later we are in the Lamborghini, rolling towards the gate in the chainlink fence. Krells working for minimum wage, stolen cars, fraudulent recycling rackets, biomodification clinics, it's all connected, I'm sure, in a tangled web that we don't want to get stuck in at any price.

We'll head for the spaceport, where *hopefully* Kenneth, Vanessa, and Ruby are still waiting for us.

I get out to deal with the gate. My lightsaber fades and dies as I hack through the hasp of the padlock. That's it for my A-tech superweapon, unless I find a fresh powerpack lying around somewhere.

Wheeeee ....

Every hair on my body stands on end. I squint upwards. I gave the sunglasses to Imogen earlier, so all I can see is the purple sky and the water in my own eyes. Then I make out a bright spot that isn't the sun.

The XS rocket boys are on the job again.

And this time we're in their crosshairs.

CHAPTER 7

The rocket tumbles and swerves through the sky, seeking its target.

Us.

Every second feels like a lifetime. I wrestle with the padlock on the scrap yard's gate. I managed to cut the hasp almost all the way through before my lightsaber died. Finally the last thread of metal snaps. I fling the padlock to the ground, kick the gate open, and fly back to the Lamborghini. "Go!" I shout, jumping into the passenger seat.

Imogen has taken Sam's place at the wheel. "Not yet," she says with zombie-like calm. Still as a snake, sensible taxi driver's shoes poised on the pedals, she stares fixedly through the windscreen at the blazing meteor that's coming for us.

"Maybe it'll detonate when it hits the fence," I mutter, not trusting Imogen's reflexes.

"And maybe it won't," Sam snarls. He didn't want to let Imogen drive 'his' Lamborghini. I had to speak quite sharply to get him to move over.

"Wait … wait … wait," Imogen mutters. Tension building,

she hunches over the wheel. The idling engine rumbles.

The rocket gets brighter and bigger and closer, painting a smoky contrail in the sky.

I'm afraid Sam may be right about the fence. The roof part is only meant to stop anti-grav-enabled vehicles, not rockets. The hexagonal gaps in it are *feet* wide. There's easily room for a high-explosive warhead to pass through.

Wheeee ...

Panic seizes me. I grab the door handle.

"Wait," Imogen chants. "Wait, wait, *wait!*"

WHEEEE screams the rocket, blazing straight down out of the sky.

At the very last possible instant, Imogen throws the Lamborghini into gear and accelerates so hard we're thrown back violently against the seats.

We smash through the gate, knocking it wide open, and soar into the air.

Behind us, the scrap yard blows up.

"OK," Imogen says in a shaky voice. "That worked. Oh my God. It actually worked." She takes off her sunglasses and tosses them into the back. She pumps both fists in the air. "We're alive!"

I grab her hands and replace them on the steering wheel. Then I plant a big kiss on her cheek. "That was flawless, Ms. Kincaid." Now that the danger is past, I'm more than willing to give her her due. That was an amazing display of nerve under pressure. All she had to do was wait until it was too late for the rocket to change course. But if you think that's easy, try it at home sometime.

Sam sags across the back seat. "Balls of steel," he says. "And reflexes like a mongoose on amphetamines."

"Um, that's not very flattering, Sam." Imogen laughs, but I'm proud of him for saying that. It almost eases my mind about our near-fatal car accident. Almost.

The scrap yard shrinks below. The fireball is already sputtering out. The rocket hit the ground, gouged out a crater, and did little damage otherwise, apart from taking a year or two off my life.

Imogen banks through the smoke rising from the scrap yard and flies over the maze city, low and fast. She hugs the landscape, jinking over the occasional fragment of wall left standing.

I pull myself together. "Sam, there should be a McDonald's bag in the back. And a couple of cans of Red Bull."

We polish off these scanty provisions—the leftovers of the last McDonald's meal Imogen bought on Arcadia, 500 lightyears away—in approximately two minutes.

The Red Bull gives me a second wind. I tap the Lamborghini's sat-nav screen. "Imogen, look at this. It's a major traffic artery. Shortest route between the spaceport and that cactus over there. Loads of cars in the air. If we merge into that, they'll have to lay off with the rockets."

"Wanna bet?" Imogen says, but she angles the Lamborghini in the direction of the artery route. I turn off the sat-nav. No sense helping them to target us again.

I don't even know if it is the electronics they've been targeting. But if they're watching us from orbit, we're screwed anyway.

The artery route glistens from afar, a line of traffic flowing through the air about 200 meters up. We join the inbound stream of vehicles making for the spaceport.

They're all makes and models, from earthmovers to family cars and school buses. Arnold is turning into a real colony. People have been coming out here on holiday for ages, and now the emigrants are starting to come. I suppose it takes all sorts. Personally I'd be annoyed by the XS Group lobbing rockets around the place, but maybe they think it's all part of the freewheeling frontier culture.

The Lamborghini doesn't stick out as badly as I was afraid of, and we complete our journey to the spaceport in record time. It's brilliant to see human buildings below, as opposed to Krell ruins. We're singing "Amazing Grace" (one of the few songs Sam knows) as Imogen sets the Lamborghini down in the corner of the spaceport parking lot.

I agree, it is a bit silly to have a parking lot on a moon that is, or will soon be, one giant parking lot. But we do not want to get stopped at this point for parking on the imaginary double yellow lines.

Sam kisses the steering wheel as he scrambles out across the driver's seat. "Goodbye, baby. Wish I could take you with me." He's cheered up again, seemingly having forgotten the aggro I gave him over the dead security guards—and the guards themselves, for that matter. That's the thing about Sam. He can literally forget that he killed two innocent people on the spur of the moment. And that's why I have to seriously consider the possibility that he tried to kill myself and Imogen, too.

It's splat in the middle of Arnold's 29-hour day now, hotter than ever. We scurry into the terminal building. The sprawling air-conditioned concourse would not be out of place on Earth. Imogen stares longingly at the restaurants and cafés. "Do we have time to grab something?"

I deliberate for all of two seconds. We left Treetop nine hours ago and it feels like nine days. The smell of fast food is making my stomach growl. "All right. You two go pick something up." I hand Imogen a plastic $100 bill, the dog-end of my final paycheck from Arcadia. "I'll see if I can find a phone shop. Meet you back here in fifteen minutes."

I spend my next-to-last $100 on a prepaid phone. Mooching out of the phone shop, I angle across the concourse and climb the low flight of stairs to the mezzanine level. A curving wall of tinted glass overlooks the landing zone. Of course, you couldn't have spaceships landing and taking off too close to the terminal, so the closest ones are mere dots in the distance. The tarmac shimmers like liquid in the sun. I dial Kenneth's number.

Ring ... ring ...

One of the dots in the distance ignites into a pinpoint blaze. It shoots straight up into the sky. Tourists point it out to their children.

Ring ... ring ...

Sunburnt kiddies dash across my path as I saunter along, waiting for Kenneth to pick up. I never wanted children of my own, but something plucks at my heart now. Their little faces are happy and bright. In their world, no one steals A-tech artefacts or gets hijacked by extreme salespersons. For them, the Arnold spaceport is a wonderland where they can jump three times as high as on Earth. For me, it's the belly of the beast. I wish I lived in their world.

"You know what to do," says Kenneth's irritating nasal voice. I hang up on his voicemail and try Vanessa.

No answer from her, either. I'm trying Ruby when I come on an interesting display. It's a slanted table with a holographic diorama of the whole spaceport on it. Each little spaceship has a callout tag glowing above it. Tourists cluster around the display, cooing in admiration as a wee ship appears ten feet in the air and drops down to land in the diorama. At the same time, a star drops out of the sky outside.

I shove through the tourists and crane over the display. Every ship at the spaceport is displayed here, and that includes the ones in long-term parking. I start at the top left corner and read every single tag.

Ruby's phone rings and rings.

No *Intergalactic Bogtrotter.*

No Lockheed-Martin F-99s at all.

They might have parked her under a false name, but they couldn't have lied about her specs. It's pretty hard to disguise a decommissioned, extensively repaired USAF fighter-bomber.

"If you've got something to say, say it," Ruby's voicemail kicks in.

"Yeah, Ruby. The *Bogtrotter's* gone. It is not here. What the fecking hell is going on?"

My voice rises on the last words. Children stare at me. A mother wraps her hands around her offspring's shoulders, as if to protect them from the big man using bad words.

"Call me back," I say, and push through the crowd, my cheeks hot.

Back down on the concourse, I spot Sam standing outside the Subway franchise, his cheeks bulging, one foot-long sandwich in his hands, another one tucked under his arm.

I'm striding towards him when a fragment of conversation freezes me.

"I'm telling you it is in this very spaceport right now!"

I never expected to hear an Irish accent on Arnold.

Homesickness stabs me like a lightsaber.

Which is fairly stupid, because I recognize the voice. It is Finian's.

CHAPTER 8

It's agony not looking. But I keep my back turned to Finian's voice. He's less likely to recognize the back of my head. My hair is longer now than when he last saw me, and I dyed it brown to impersonate Baron Short.

"If you want to recover the artefact, you'll let me do my bleeding job," he says—snarls, rather, in the tone that once made bold pirates shake in their boots.

My brain's writhing in panic, but my legs keep moving and they carry me towards the Pizza Hut two shops down from the Subway franchise, where I pretend to be standing in line. With a hundred or so punters in between me and Finian, I finally allow myself to look in his direction.

He's standing with a half-dozen of his officers, all of them resplendent in their NEPD uniforms, chatting to a little besuited fella whom I take to be something to do with the spaceport.

I'm now too far away to hear what they're saying, but I recognize the way Finian is looming over the poor wee man and I estimate he'll seize him by the throat any minute. I pray the little fella can stand up to him. It's pretty clear that

Finian wants to use the powers vested in him—meaning shouting and hitting people with batons—to search the spaceport, and the wee fella is objecting on the grounds of basic decency and tourism revenues.

I sidle urgently towards Sam. I've just caught his eye when my prepaid phone rings.

I gape at it for a moment and then pick up. "Hello?"

"Who is this?"

"Ruby?"

"Yeah. Is that Fletch?"

"Where are you? We're at the spaceport, and the fecking ship isn't here."

Sam's at my shoulder now, listening in. At *the ship isn't here* he yells out, "Shit!" and I desperately shush him, jerking my thumb in Finian's direction.

"No," says Ruby. His voice is flat. "No, it isn't there."

"What the feck happened? Where are you?"

"What happened is Kenneth and his girlfriend took off with the ship."

The words send me into a mental tailspin. I feel like I've been tossed into space without an EVA suit.

I knew Kenneth was a former pirate and I knew Vanessa was more loyal to him than to us, but I thought the promise of a share in the Gizmo would keep them on-side.

Evidently I was wrong. After all, if greed is all that motivates your friends, they're not really your friends, are they?

"They took off last week," Ruby goes on. "I left the ship to do some last-minute shopping, and they launched before I even reached the terminal. I wrote you, but I guess you didn't get my letter."

The interstellar mail packets are slow. "No."

"They're probably planning to sell the ship on Flea Market. They won't get that much for it. But something's better than nothing, right?"

"Right."

"So did the operation pan out?"

"Sort of."

"Dude, it's either yes or no, it did or it didn't. The Gizmo of Rejuvenation is not freaking Schrodinger's cat. You either have it or you don't."

"Yes, we have it, but—"

"Awesome," Ruby says, perking up. "Take that, oh ye of little faith."

"But we've actually got a problem at the moment." I don't give him time to ask what it is. "I'll call you back. Where are you, anyway?"

"Flower Lake. It's this resort."

I hang up without bothering to ask Ruby what he is doing at a holiday resort.

Sam is staring dropjawed across the concourse. The confrontation between Finian and the spaceport officials seems to be escalating.

"Sam, where's Imogen?"

"She went to Starbucks."

Thank God, Starbucks is in the other direction from Finian and his men. "Come on."

"How'd he get here?" Sam walks sideways, unable to tear his eyes off the horrible sight of the NEPD squadron.

"In a ship, I suppose."

"Figure he's after us?"

"Yes, that would be my assumption," I snarl.

"But what about the Krells? It was them who set off the burglar alarm at King Zuck's. We don't even know that anyone knows the Gizmo is missing."

For the hundredth time, I brush my fingers over the outline of the Gizmo, making sure it's still in my pocket. "You could be right. But if he gets his hands on us, he'll know the Gizmo is missing then, won't he?"

We plunge into Starbucks. It's crowded. Imogen has an unaccountable passion for frappuccino. There she is, waiting at the counter where the drinks are delivered.

"Imogen." She twitches as Sam and I suddenly appear on either side of her. "Bad news: Finian's here. We've got to leg it."

"But I'm still waiting for my drink," she says.

I know it's going to take a few moments for it to sink in. A person cannot react immediately to news this crushingly bad. Unfortunately, we don't have a few moments. I fasten my hand around her arm. Her eyes darken.

Sam stiffens. "Oh shit." I follow his gaze to the entrance.

Finian's shoving his way into the shop, flanked by his men. Raising his flashing baton to attract attention, he booms, "Near Earth Police Department! Remain calm and nobody will get hurt!"

The three of us edge behind the freestanding shelves of souvenir mugs and doodads. These are high enough to conceal us from the NEPD for at least a moment. My eyes dart, plotting an escape route: through the seating area, nip behind their backs, and away; he might not even notice us, he's so busy intimidating the populace—

"Imogen!" A barista slams a plastic cup on the counter. "Imogen, your venti mocha frappuccino with extra mocha and caramel is READY!'"

Why does she have to have such a rare name?

Finian lets out a roar and charges.

His men follow, batons whirling.

They get entangled with a flock of pensioners towing suitcases bigger than they are.

I drag Imogen behind the Starbucks counter. She snags her drink on the way.

"Sorry, sorry, excuse me—"

Back into the storage area. Baristas on their break are eating enormous muffins, surrounded by boxes of coffee.

"Which way out?"

A barista gestures mutely with a muffin.

We crash through a steel door into a service corridor. Sam, on our heels, is laughing wildly. I will later learn that he tipped over a coffee machine on his way behind the counter, complicating Finian's passage and probably giving several baristas third-degree burns.

We sprint along the corridor, dodging service workers. Imogen is still holding onto her frappuccino, one hand over the lid so it won't spill.

"Back to the Lamborghini," I yell.

"But what about the *Bogtrotter?*" Imogen gasps.

Oh Christ, I haven't told her that part yet. "Kenneth and Vanessa stole her. She's probably in a hundred pieces on Flea Market by now."

Imogen wails in despair, inasmuch as one can when running flat out.

"Cheer up," I pant. "She was at the end of her days, anyway. The insurance payments were more than she was worth."

At the end of the corridor, an emergency exit door beckons. I crash the push-bar down. A klaxon erupts. We stumble out into the sunlight, which seems brighter than ever. The heat feels hotter than ever. At least we're in shadow.

We've come out on a different side of the terminal from where we went in. This appears to be a service parking area. Beyond the parked vans and lorries, a mountain of demolition debris rises to the sky.

An explosion shakes the still air. We flinch back against the terminal building.

"Was that a ship taking off?" Imogen says.

"It didn't sound like that," I say.

People are clambering down the rubble mountain. They're wearing business suits, slipping and sliding on the chunks of pulverized Krell buildings.

"Those are stackers," Imogen says unexpectedly.

"You can tell?" I say.

"*Uccchh.* I used to work with those people, remember? Bet you anything they're Big Tech guys."

"In that case, I certainly don't want to meet them."

We scuttle along the side of the terminal, staying in the building's narrow strip of shadow.

Up on top of the debris mound, a radio crackles loudly.

I glance back. More figures are descending the rubble. Feck! They're NEPD officers, helmeted and jackbooted. They overtake the suits and knock one of them over. The suits shout at them and they shout back.

"Run," I say.

We sprint to the corner of the terminal building. I break stride for another glance back.

The NEPD officers have almost reached the bottom of the rubble mountain, slithering as fast as they can. But that's not the worst thing I see.

From this vantage, I can see the sloping summit of the rubble mountain. And up there in the sunlight stands a skeletal jeep, painted in the NEPD colors. There's a frame over the back of the jeep that supports a contraption like a very large milk bottle, angled towards the sky.

I've seen one of those before, on the Draco spur.

It's a rocket launcher.

We break into the sunlight. I'm out of breath, pouring with sweat. Families and tour groups meander across the visitor parking lot, shaded by parasols, portable fans whirring.

I seize Imogen's hand and drag her straight through a tour group. They exclaim in shock at our rudeness.

"Sam!" Imogen cries.

I look back. Sam's sprawled full length on the tarmac. He must have tripped in those over-large sneakers he borrowed from the dead Krell security guard.

The NEPD officers are closing in.

I hesitate.

Imogen doesn't.

She dashes back, screams at the closest officer, and throws her frappuccino into his face.

By that time I've dragged Sam to his feet. We run for the Lamborghini, Sam limping—it turns out he lost one sneaker in Starbucks and the bottom of his bare foot is torn to ribbons. That doesn't stop him laughing. "That was awesome, Imogen! A frappuccino bomb! I fucking love it!"

The NEPD officers have stopped to help their colleague,

who is screaming his head off, maybe thinking he's been doused with acid or something. We zigzag behind the cars and buses to the Lamborghini.

It's been sitting in the sun so the inside is like an oven. While they're opening all the doors, I get into the driver's seat.

Sam is still laughing and Imogen's smiling primly. "I really wanted that frappuccino," she says.

"I'll buy you another when we get off-planet," Sam says. "I'll buy you a whole fucking Starbucks franchise."

"Buy yourself a pair of shoes first."

I'm in no mood to join in their laughter. The situation is still extremely hairy. I gun the engine, roll out of our parking place, and take off.

The NEPD officers below glance up at us and then go on searching the parking lot. It does not occur to them that we may be in possession of a pricey sports car. And from down there they can't see the crumpled bonnet.

"Where are we going, anyway?" Imogen says. She goes on without waiting for me to reply. "The way I see it, we've got to lie low for a while. The NEPD are doofuses. They'll go away. But what about Maude's gang? Shit shit *shit.*"

"That just about sums it up," I say. "But we'll worry about all that after we pick Ruby up."

I expect protests from them both and I get them aplenty. Neither Sam nor Imogen is friends with Ruby. Imogen only met him on the Lost Planet, when Ruby was whining and moaning every waking minute about how he didn't quit his job at Goldman Sachs for *this*. Then when we got back to Arcadia she was working as a taxi driver and he was waiting tables at a nightclub, so they hardly ever saw each other. Sam used to go to Ruby's nightclub occasionally and laugh at his pretensions. Ruby is transitioning to female. He had to stop taking his meds after the Lost Planet debacle, as we had no money, so he's been stuck in an awful in-between stage for a while—a transvestite with stubble. Some people find that laughable or perverse. I have been among them at times. Well, quite often. But that doesn't justify abandoning him, after Kenneth and Vanessa have abandoned him already.

Basically, I have to start doing the right thing at some stage, or there won't be anything left of me.

I can't say that out loud, of course. It would ruin my image. I just point out, "Ruby would turn us in in a heartbeat if Finian catches him."

"Oh, dammit," Sam sighs. "In that case, I suppose we have to bump him off."

"Sam!" Imogen says.

"Just kidding, just kidding." Sam gives us one of his lazy smiles. "I meant to say rescue him from whatever hole he's hiding in. Did he say?"

I lean forward and speak into the sat-nav. "Flower Lake."

It's not that far, thank feck.

"Flower Lake," Sam says. "I've never heard of it."

"Nor have I. It's some kind of resort."

We fly over the built-up area outside the spaceport. I keep the speed to the legal limit, and watch other cars hurtle gaily past at twice that.

"Aren't you going to turn the GPS off?" Sam says.

"The sat-nav? I'm using it."

"I thought you said they could use it to track us."

"That was when I thought it was the XS Group shooting rockets at us."

"Wasn't it?"

"No, you idjit. It was Finian. Did you not see that set-up in the service parking area?"

"Oh."

"The NEPD's jurisdiction ends at the perimeter of the spaceport. The tech lobby squeezed that concession out of the pols, to make sure there'd be no interference with the various profit-making activities out here. So what does the auld bastard do but he brings along his truck-mounted rocket launcher to extend his range?"

"So how *were* they targeting us?" Sam says.

"Fecked if I know." I touch the outline of the Gizmo once more. "I thought there might be a transmitter dot on the Gizmo, but I had a good look at it. There isn't."

"Oh," Imogen says.

"What?" Sam and I say at once, because there's that note of consternation in her voice that you might hear when terrible news has been received.

"Um, I …" In the mirror, she's pink, and I don't think it's just the sunburn. "I might know how they're tracking us."

She works one hand into the pocket of her tight taxi driver's trousers, and opens her fist to reveal a tangle of wires and cloudy crystals.

The Krell artefact.

CHAPTER 9

Look on the bright side, I tell myself. At least she came clean about it.

"Nice job, Ms. Kincaid," I say. "How did you pull it off?"

Defensively, she says, "The Krells were dead. It was just lying there." She shrugs. "I took it."

This puts a new color on the way she left the recycling center and ran off across the desert. With this in her pocket, she must have thought she didn't need us anymore. I don't know whether to be glad or angry that she changed her mind.

Sam grabs the artefact. Imogen doesn't try to stop him. He holds it up to the window. "Aha. GPS dot."

So I had the right idea. Wrong artefact.

And we might have found that GPS dot much earlier if Imogen had told us she had the artefact, or if she'd even looked at it properly.

"Are you going to throw it away?" Imogen says.

"Oh, maybe," I say. "It always gives me a kick to toss millions of dollars out of the window. No, of course we're not throwing it away."

"I can get this off," Sam says, scraping at the GPS dot with his thumbnail. "There."

He peels the remains of his left sock off, wraps the GPS dot in the bloodstained terrycloth, and rolls down the window. The car fills with the throb of air. Sam hurls the sock and the GPS dot out, and rolls the window up again..

"Look for a missile to land in that area soon," he says.

"It's an hour's drive," I say. "You two might as well get some sleep."

Imogen curls up on the back seat. I'm sure she's not really asleep. She's mourning.

Sam takes his other shoe off and props his bare feet on the dashboard. He turns the mess of flimsy wires and crystals in his hands. "How hard you think it'd be to reverse-engineer this?"

"No idea. Sam, there's just too much A-tech in the galaxy. If you try to figure out how it all works you'll go mad."

"But this thing might be a goldmine. That dude said the Krells used it to swim underwater. We could make a fortune selling cheap copies on the Beach."

The Beach is another misleadingly named planet which is all water. A few people live there in seasteads.

"We don't even know that he was right," I say, remembering the thief with pity. "The poor fella was unbalanced. He was probably just guessing."

"Maybe there was a label on the display case."

"There were no labels on any of the exhibits." I shake my head. "It could be an aqualung, an extension cord, or the key to the seventh seal of the fecking apocalypse. We don't know how the Krells thought."

"We don't know how any of them thought," Sam

acknowledges.

Imogen speaks up from the back seat. I knew she wasn't asleep. "Reverse-engineering A-tech is basically a process of working out how dead aliens thought. You have to get into their heads to understand their technology."

"My mom spent nine years trying to work out how the Denebites thought," Sam says. "She failed."

His mother, Special Delivery Sam, ended up getting arrested for her crimes on the Omega Centauri spur. They sent the military after her. It was the first-ever military operation outside our own solar system, which gives you an idea of just how heinous her crimes were. Finian got caught in the same net. He was trying to kill Special Delivery Sam at the time, which probably told in his favor. He ended up in the NEPD. She ended up in a maximum-security prison on Earth. Sam's never given any indication of being upset about that. He'd already cut his own ties with her, after all. But now something in his voice makes me wonder how he really feels about it all.

"Here." He passes the Krell artefact back to Imogen. "It's probably just jewelry or something."

We fly over the demolished region of the maze city, and then a non-demolished region, and then a human industrial cluster, and finally a cactus town. This would be where the school buses and SUVs in the air are coming from. There are caves in the sides of the cactus. People have dug holes in the giant plant and trained it to grow back around nanowire frames, forming smooth cavities. It's a bit like a pueblo of old, with strips of cultivated sunflowers and roses outside. They tap the cactus itself for water.

I fly up over the side of the cactus. The sat-nav says

Flower Lake is on the *top* of here, which seems like a queer place to build a holiday resort. I hug the knolls and valleys of the gargantuan plant, flying low—because I'm still feeling paranoid—and slow—because I'm not the driver Imogen is.

The lumps and bumps become steeper. The shadow of the Lamborghini glides over crevices Swiss-cheesed with burrows. I wonder what kind of creatures come out of there at night? My imagination suggests scorpion-analogs and rattlesnake-analogs. I'm starting to hate this moon, and the Krells who designed it.

"Look," I say. "No more spikes."

We are now flying over waves of thin, frilly ridges gradated from pale green to white. "Weird," Sam says without interest.

Suddenly the cactus drops away. Ahead glitters a plain of ... *water!*

Tall, slender poles poke out of the water, attracting swarms of insects so dense they look like black clouds. Rainbow-colored birds flock on the surface. The entire depression in the cactus is rimmed with knife-edged ridges like the ones we just flew over, so thin at the tops that the sun shines through them. Around the shores of the lake, fan-like growths crowd in splashes of orange and pink, shading the shallows.

Imogen sits up. "Oh, cool!" she says. "Flower Lake! Duh! I've heard of these! Guys, we are *inside* a cactus flower. That's nectar, and oh my God, there are people swimming in it!"

There are indeed. Watching them splash and float on lilos with attached parasols, my whole body thirsts for the embrace of water. Nectar? Water? I don't care as long as it's wet. I'm hot and sticky and tired and a dip would be the best thing in the world just now.

The swimmers are diving off a pier, clearly manmade, that juts out into the lake. Beyond it, a collection of rustic buildings sprawls along the shore. The swimmers are not paying any attention to the Lamborghini buzzing over their heads, because there is a parking lot attached to the complex, and it is half full of cars already.

"I'm putting down in the carpark over there," I say.

Sam frowns. "Fletch, we don't know what this place is. I don't like going in with no information."

I exhale through my nose. If he was going to quibble, could he not have done it earlier? All right, he *did* do it earlier, and I overruled him. I'll just have to do it again. As tactfully as possible.

"It is a holiday resort," I say. "You're from Omega Centauri, Sam, so you're not always au fait with trends on Earth. But people from Earth like taking holidays on other planets. Arnold is cheap and you can make day trips to Treetop for the shopping. I always thought it was only suckers who plunked down for Arnold tours, but now I admit that I may have been mistaken, because this looks very nice indeed. Anyway, this is where Ruby is. Call him." I flip Sam my prepaid.

He dials and waits while I set the Lamborghini down in the parking lot.

"No answer," he says as we get out.

I don't reply immediately, testing the springy cactus-stuff underfoot. It's cooler up here. The air, however, seems richer. Maybe the tall petals swaying around the parking lot somehow emit oxygen. They cast sharp shadows. There's an elusive, tangy scent in the air that reminds me of juniper.

A valet hurries up, wearing a loose white uniform with a sunhat tied under her chin. "Hi! Do you have a reservation?"

I step in front of the other two and give her my widest, most charming smile. "We do not, but I was hoping you'd take walk-ins."

"Well, it depends on which package you're thinking of. But we would definitely hope to accommodate you, so if I could just have your names?" She gets out a tablet.

"Certainly, and as to the package, what do you recommend?" I am winging this. Hope I don't end up committing us to aromatherapy massages or anything of that sort.

A plump, pink-faced body with 'manager' practically written on his forehead is hurrying across the parking-lot. I wait for him to reach us before continuing.

"My name is Dick Short—Lord Short of Pervée—and this is my good friend Baron Hofacker of Zabordelo."

It's amazing the effect that titles have on people, even when they're obviously self-service ones. The manager instantly digests the information that *these people own planets.* He gains two inches in height. "It is a pleasure to host you at Flower Lake, your lordships, and …?" He smiles at Imogen.

"My fiancée," I purr. Sometimes the devil gets into me. I can't help it.

"A pleasure, my lady. If you'd like to come this way to our reception area …"

Before we set out on our ill-fated trip up the Beta Aurigae

spur, we took the *Skint Idjit* on a cargo run out to Hell's Armpit—another misnamed planet. It's gorgeous there. We stayed one night in a mansion owned by the CFO of Google. You could hardly tell if you were inside or outside. Everything was open to nature, with birds flying around and plants growing through the floors.

The foyer of the Flower Lake resort reminds me of that, except all the plants are spikier. We recline in huge wicker chairs and sip cold drinks. Mine's a Pepsi.

Guests wander through the foyer in swimsuits. They stare curiously at us. I can't blame them—we're a sight: Sam in a tuxedo shirt and security guard's trousers; Imogen in her taxi driver's uniform, minus the blazer; and me still dressed as a waiter. But so what? Aristocrats can wear whatever they like.

"When I have my own planet, I think I'll call myself *Taoiseach,*" I muse. "King is too common, and I'm bored of Baron."

"What does Teeshuck mean?" Imogen says. She's got a frappuccino-style drink in her hand. It seems to have cheered her up.

"It's Irish for President."

Imogen chokes on her coffee. "I'm trying to imagine you going into politics."

"What do you mean? We had a Taoiseach at one stage who was a convicted arms dealer and was involved in serious real estate fraud. He was a moustache away from being a Bond villain. And people *still* say he was the best Taoiseach we ever had."

Imogen giggles. It feels good that I can still make her laugh.

My grin fades. "But it doesn't matter anyway, because

there won't be any other people on my planet."

The manager comes back, tablet in hand. "Thank you very much, your lordships, you ladyship. Now regarding payment, would you like to make a deposit of ten percent or twenty-five percent? We accept cash only, I'm afraid."

A while back there was a movement to do away with cash altogether, on the basis that ne'er-do-wells use cash, whereas decent people use credit. The privacy advocates won that one. Right now, I wish they hadn't. As Baron Short, I've got a five-figure credit line (which has to be repaid to the Russians). But I've only $102 in my pocket.

Aristocrats always carry cash. If I reveal how broke I am, it'll blow our cover.

"Look, to be honest, all we want is a club sandwich and half an hour on the computer."

"And a swim," Imogen pipes up.

"Can we not do this a la carte, as it were?"

Hark to Fletch the planet-owner.

I never find out if we would have got away with it or not, because at that moment I spot Ruby, wearing a loose white uniform, coming out of the elevator with a stack of towels.

CHAPTER 10

I wouldn't have known it was Ruby if I wasn't expecting to see him here. He really looks like a woman! The five o'clock shadow is gone, the face is narrower—almost triangular—and the swaying walk emphasizes wider hips.

But it *is* him. I'm out of my chair like a shot, leaving Imogen to deal with the manager. I accost Ruby before he can vanish through the swinging doors to the pier.

He jumps three feet in the air and drops his stack of towels.

"Was that you in the Lamborghini?"

"I am a baron, you know."

Credit where it's due, Ruby can think on his feet. He's a stacker. Maybe I should say he used to be a stacker. It's the nootropic drugs they take that really give them their edge, and he had to go off those. They cost a bundle and every penny we were making on Arcadia was going to the Russian fake-ID vendors. But he's still got his genetically boosted IQ, and he spins the manager a whole fable about how he personally invited us to experience Flower Lake for the afternoon before we return to our planets in the Perseus arm. He seems to have a fair amount of credibility with the manager. We squeak through on promises that we'll talk the place up to our planet-owning friends.

We get loaner swimsuits so we'll be in compliance with the dress code. Imogen finishes her coffee and goes in swimming. I manage with great difficulty to persuade Sam to do the same. He stays bobbing around nearby, sprawled on one of their lilos with the attached parasols. But the lapping of the water against the pier and the droning of the insects, which drifts across the lake from the nearest pistil stalks, reassures me that he can't overhear our conversation.

"Ruby, I'm concerned about him." It's a huge relief to spill it out. "He tried to run me and Imogen over in the Lamborghini."

Ruby's eyes open wide. We have filled him in about our adventures on the way here, but of course I didn't mention our near-fatal car accident while Sam was listening. "Are you sure?" he says.

"Of course I'm not sure. But if I wait to be sure, I'll be dead. He wants the Gizmo."

"Color me unsurprised," Ruby says. "It's worth billions."

Billions of dollars currently folded up, in a hidden dimension as it were, in my trousers, which I'm sitting on. I had to change into this horrible Speedo on account of the dress code, but I'm not letting the trousers out of my sight. The Gizmo is a lump under my left buttock.

"Well, what do you want to do about him?" Ruby says.

We both look at Sam. He's dabbling his feet in the water and drinking beer.

"I don't know," I say, suddenly feeling like a coward and a fool. "I was hoping you'd have some ideas."

Ruby used to kill people. He tried to kill me once, and he very nearly did kill Donal. But that was when he worked for Goldman Sachs. Now he doesn't even look like the same person anymore. He doesn't *sound* like the same person. He's done something to his voicebox.

He shakes his head. "I want no part of this, Fletch." He brushes his hair out of his eyes, a very feminine gesture.

"Your Adam's apple's gone," I say, noticing.

"Yeah, and did you see my jawline?" He turns his head and touches the corner of his jaw just below his ear. It's less pronounced than it used to be. The whole shape of his face looks different. "They've got some great surgeons here. First-class professionals."

Ruby has explained to us all that he started working here after Kenneth and Vanessa stole the *Bogtrotter*, leaving him flat. "I'd already come out here a couple of times to buy drugs, and I'd developed a rapport with the manager, so he was happy to offer me a position—" this is how Ruby talks. For him, Jacob Ruby is the center of the universe and we're all just shadows on the wall. It's extraordinary how stackers can maintain their egocentric confidence even when life repeatedly kicks them in the goolies.

I glance at Ruby's groin, concealed by the loose white folds of his uniform. He catches me looking and proffers a close-lipped smile. Has he still got all his bits, or did the surgeons of Flower Lake rid him of those, too? I can't guess and you couldn't pay me enough to ask.

"So why have they got surgeons here, anyway, Ruby? Is that one of the packages? Go on holiday and come back as the opposite sex?"

"Yeah, and they also do facelifts, liposuction, etcetera,"

Ruby says. He nods at the clients sitting at the other tables on the pier, sipping drinks beneath big parasols. Many of them wear bandages, ranging from single eyepatches to the full Egyptian mummy look.

"And you're happy working here?"

Ruby nods. "To be totally honest with you, Fletch? This is the first time I've felt at peace with myself in God, I don't even know how long."

It's completely ridiculous but my eyes suddenly prickle with tears. I take a big bite of my club sandwich to hide it.

"I've put up with being demeaned and insulted for years. Like my whole adult life, actually, going back to when I worked for GS. But here? Everyone's cool. It's a community of outsiders. For the first time in my life, I fit in. You probably can't even imagine how that feels."

I'm about to say no, I can't, but then I suddenly remember that I do know how it feels. I took it for granted when I lived at home in Lisdoonvarna. Ruby may never have had that experience in his over-privileged, rackety life.

"So yeah. There's no easy way to say this, but Fletch … I'm out. Sorry. You'll just have to go on to Pervée without me."

He looks uncomfortable. In his egocentric way, he assumes this will be a devastating blow.

"Of course, I'll relinquish my share of the proceeds," he adds.

Well, I should hope so.

Unfortunately, leaving that aside, this *is* a devastating blow. I was counting on Ruby to figure out how we're going to get off this bloody moon. And to help me decide what to do about Sam.

I force a smile. "As long as you're happy."

"I am. I am." His gaze flits past me. "Well, nothing's perfect," he says wryly.

I'm on a hair trigger at this point and as soon as I realize he's looking at something or someone behind me, I twist around.

A new group of clients has sat down at the table nearest ours. They poke at the menu tablet, chattering in Chinese.

They are Krells.

My jaw hits the floor. "Jesus! What are *they* doing here?"

"House specialty," Ruby says. "Transgender is so old hat." He sounds a bit annoyed not to be on the cutting edge. "Transspecies is the next big thing."

I shake my head. "Transspecies has been the next big thing for the last twenty years. Don't you remember Woolly?"

Woolly was our pilot on the *Skint Idjit*. She'd had the surgery to turn herself into a facsimile of a wookie.

"Yeah, sure, but wookies never actually existed. Krells did."

"So?"

"So the technology's finally getting to the point where they can do these more extreme transitions."

I stiffen, suddenly remembering dead bodies in the back of a recycling truck. The vulture-analogs had eaten so much of their faces that I couldn't tell if they were baseline humans or not. "Ruby? How good are these surgeons really?"

"Like I said, they're really good."

"But are they good enough to get it right every time? This technology is still in its infancy, correct? And it's based on

A-tech. That's always somewhat experimental. Are they good enough that no one ever dies on the operating table?"

Ruby looks unhappy. "I don't know, Fletch. That's way above my pay grade."

I think he does know, and just doesn't want to admit it, because that would mean admitting that his cool community of outsiders has a dark side. In fact, a lethal side. So I say it for him. "I think they do die, Ruby. I think a fair number of them die, and the bodies are put into a recycling incinerator, and the risks don't even make it into the fine print of the brochures that the salespeople hand out at fancy parties."

Ruby throws up his hands. "What do you want me to do about it?"

I shake my head. "Nothing." I'm tenser than ever, scanning the whole pier. Just because I can't see any danger doesn't mean it's not there. "Just tell me this. Does Flower Lake ever use salespeople from the XS Group?"

CHAPTER 11

"There are a dozen health resorts like this on Arnold," Ruby says. "If your hijackers really were XS Group salespeople, they came from someplace else."

"Except this resort's quite close to where that demented cow put us down."

"Fletch, you have to be careful with that kind of language around here. This isn't the Beta Aurigae spur."

I stand up to survey the pier. I can see only the one group of Krells. The others are probably hidden away in their rooms, recuperating from surgery. Or in bags, waiting to be picked up for recycling. What drives people to take these kinds of risks, only to end up looking like bipedal natterjack toads?

I suddenly recall something. "Ruby, the security guards at the scrap yard were Krells."

"Oh yes," he says. "Flower Lake offers an instalment plan for clients with limited means. That's actually how I'm paying for my surgeries. They let you work off the costs over a period of time."

"That proves it, then. The resort's affiliated with that

scrap yard. That's where the XS Group had our taxi towed. And it's only on the other side of this cactus."

"Proves what? Tell me, Fletch, exactly what that proves." Ruby's getting cross now.

"It proves that we have to leg it this very fecking second," I mutter. "The manager probably rang Maude the second he saw the Lamborghini."

I squint out into the lake, trying to identify Imogen among the scattered swimmers. Sam paddles his lilo back towards the pier. "What's up, Fletch?"

With difficulty, I hide my panic. "Ah, I was just trying to see where Imogen went. Can you see her at all?"

"I think that's her over there," he says, gesturing vaguely. "You gonna go in?"

"Sure, why don't you come with me? We should look for her. She's been in a while."

Sam caws a laugh. "Dude. I can't swim."

"I thought Omega Centauri 49 was a wet planet."

"Wet as in it rains a lot. Do you go in swimming when it's raining?"

"Yes. I'm Irish."

"Well, I'm not, and anyway, I'm starving." Sam loops the tether of his lilo onto the post attached to the steps. "Ruby, do we get free food? Or were the free drinks the extent of it?"

I glance at my folded trousers.

Sam comes up the steps and starts flicking through the menu, while Ruby irritably tells him not to order the most expensive thing.

I place my shoes and socks on top of my trousers. I'll just have to chance it.

"Going to look for Imogen," I say, and dive off the pier.

Whew! The water embraces my body with a glorious shock. It's cold, sure. But when you come from the west coast of Ireland, it's fine to go in as long as there's not actually ice on the surface.

I get a little water in my mouth, and remember it's not actually water, it's cactus nectar. It is ever so slightly sweet.

I don't feel buoyant, either. It's more like swimming in a pond than in the sea. That makes sense.

I break into a crawl, heading for the clump of swimmers I saw from the pier.

But it turns out that none of them are Imogen. They're Australians, here to have everything lifted and tucked. They tell me that they thought at first I was one of the Krells. "That lot are always swimming underwater. Bloody creepy!" They're nice ladies but they haven't seen Imogen, and I strike off again into the lake.

Could something have happened to her? I can't see her anywhere, although it's not a perfect view with the lilos floating around, and the pistil stalks protruding from the water, each one veiled in its own cloud of buzzing insects.

I glance back at the pier. A waiter is delivering a whole tray full of food to Sam. That should keep him busy for a while.

I decide to swim in a big circle around the pier. This time I try swimming with my head underwater and my eyes open.

Holy feck! I can see all the way to the bottom. This is amazing!

The water's perfectly clear. Purple and pink pond weed covers the bottom, and little fish-analogs dart around in it.

Those Krells certainly did a righteous job of terraforming

this place. How could biomodified humans ever measure up? If you looked like a Krell but weren't a Krell, wouldn't it just give you an even worse inferiority complex?

Brushing these fruitless speculations away, I swim in a breaststroke so as to splash less, coming up for air every couple of strokes. I'm looking for Imogen's drowned body on the bottom. I'm looking for an excuse to stop running. I'm looking for a way out of my life.

Without warning, someone grabs my legs and pulls me under.

I kick wildly, and break free. Spinning in a cloud of bubbles, I find myself looking into Imogen's smiling face. Her eyes and her mouth are open. She shouts: "How fucking cool is this?" and I can hear her. Underwater, I can hear her.

Her hair's held back with an arrangement of wires that loops over her face like a dog's muzzle, and there are two small gray things stuck in her nostrils, and more of the wires vanish into her mouth.

I latch my hand into her swimsuit and kick for the surface. It's hard to pull her up into the air. She doesn't want to come. When I finally get her to break the surface, she bucks violently and spews water from her mouth. She retches several times, expelling the water that filled her lungs.

Normally, a person whose lungs were filled with water is drowned.

"It's the Krell artefact, isn't it?"

She's sneezed out the crystals that were in her nose. Now she spits out another one from her mouth. She floats on her back with the artefact tangled in her hair. "Yes, and thanks for spoiling my swim, asshole."

"It really works," I say stupidly.

"Apparently so. The Krells weren't amphibian, after all. They just had very advanced scuba diving equipment."

"Now we know why that biomodder risked going to jail for it," I say, thinking aloud. "We can sell that for an easy five figures. It's just a toy, really. But it's all about the supply and demand ..."

Imogen wrenches the artefact off her head, throws it at me. I catch it just before it sinks into the depths. "I knew you guys were going to screw me over," she says bitterly. "That's why I took it."

"Imogen—"

"You don't trust me, and that's fine. I know I haven't earned your trust."

I want to listen to her, but my attention's divided. Back on the pier, the waiter clears away Sam's plate. Ruby's gone. He must have had to go back to work. I'm treading water, getting tired.

"So it's just like, what's the use? They're never going to trust me, so why should I even bother playing fair?"

The droning of the insects thickens into a rumble. I glance up. The stubby rocket shape of a car passes overhead and circles in to land in the Flower Lake parking lot. The sunlight reflects off the paintwork, turning it colorless. What would it say on the side, anyway? THE XS GROUP in big bright lettering?

"Imogen—"

On the pier, Sam stands up and strolls away, a bundle of folded cloth over his arm. I immediately forget about the car.

"SAM'S RUNNING AWAY WITH MY TROUSERS!"

We swim back to the pier as fast as we can. In between gasping breaths, I tell Imogen that I've been watching Sam ever since we left Treetop. I've suspected that he would double-cross us if he got a chance, for what does he owe us really? Nothing. We're the ones who invaded the Omega Centauri spur and indirectly caused his mother to get slung into jail. Why would he share the proceeds of the Gizmo with us if he had a chance to do otherwise? His friendly act is just that, an act. It means no more than his decision to dress up for the party as James Bond.

"Jesus, the nerve of the man!" I explode, hauling myself up the steps of the pier. My legs are rubbery. "He even sat down and ate lunch before walking off with the loot!"

As we hurry past the table where Sam was sitting, I see that he's even left a fecking tip.

He's also left my shoes behind. I suppose they were too big for him.

I go back and put them on, while Imogen dances with impatience. "Where's he gone?"

"The Lamborghini, of course."

"He hasn't got the keys!"

"Those were in my trousers, too."

We blow through the foyer. There's no one there. That strikes me as a bad sign.

I push open the door to the parking lot.

Crack!

A single gunshot echoes across the parking lot, and the glass door bows out and hits me in the face.

CHAPTER 12

I sit down hard on the foyer floor. The door bends and flexes as bullets hit the glass and bounce off. It's not breaking, because it's *not* glass, it's some amazing A-tech stuff that absorbs kinetic energy.

"Your nose is bleeding!" Imogen says.

"Thank feck that's all that's bleeding." I glance around the foyer. We're still alone, and no wonder. Someone's just opened up on the hotel with a machine-gun.

I'd be hiding too if the Gizmo weren't somewhere out there.

I wipe blood off my upper lip with the back of my hand. Imogen shrugs her shirt on over her swimsuit, jams her feet into her shoes. "Who's shooting?" she hisses, during a lull.

"Sam didn't have a gun, so that leaves Maude. The manager must have rung her to say the Lamborghini turned up in the possession of three fake aristocrats."

I crawl up to the door and push it a few inches open, keeping my head down. Warm air washes in. No more bullets come.

"I'll distract her. You stay out of sight. See if you can

reach Sam. Don't get hurt."

Imogen nods, determination in her eyes.

Then she stands up. As she steps over me, she reaches down and squeezes my shoulder.

She walks out of the door.

"Maude!" Her voice is clear and confident. "Hey girl, it's me!"

I lie unmoving for a second, stunned. A demonic thought whispers to me that she's changed sides. Walking across the parking lot, singing out Maude's name, she's hopping from our wrecked gravy train to a better, high-speed, corporate model—just as she did on the Lost Planet.

But then I remember the way she squeezed my shoulder.

And I start to crawl.

There's a hedge of giant petals along the back of the hotel building. They grow seamlessly out of the cactus, with prickly sepals at their bases. I crawl behind these to the corner of the fence. A row of cars are parked with their noses to the fence. The Lamborghini, I recall, is at the end of this row. The first car's a Porsche. The clients of this place are really well-heeled. I remember the nice Australian ladies I met swimming—why do they put up with gunfire erupting here, there, and everywhere? The answer comes with the next beat of my racing heart. Because this is Arnold, not Earth. This is how it's always been on the frontier. Now the rot's creeping inwards, and everyone's getting used to it.

I crawl under the Porsche and peek out between the rear wheels.

Imogen stands in the middle of the parking lot, looking around.

In the silence, I hear the droplets of blood from my nose splashing onto the cactus.

"Wow. Hey there," says Maude, not her real name.

Imogen jumps.

Maude walks out from behind a bus on the other side of the parking lot. She's dressed in green camouflage, carrying an assault rifle with a fancy scope. "Imogen, wasn't it? Last seen shooting my partner in the face."

"Yeah, so that went really badly," Imogen says. Her voice shakes. "But I do want to say I'm sorry. That was way out of line."

Maude laughs, dryly. "Oh hey, don't worry about it. He was a loser. It was his fault those retards stole the A-tech thingy; he wasn't watching them like he should've been."

"Gotcha," Imogen says uncertainly. "Do you want it back? The A-tech thingy." She holds it out.

Maude laughs. She comes up to Imogen, takes the artefact from her hands, and gently arranges it on top of Imogen's wet hair like a tiara. "You keep it. It's falling to pieces, anyway."

Imogen touches the wires, looking devastated.

"I was just looking for those other asshats who were with you." Maude raises her gun to her shoulder and scans the parking lot through the scope. The way she moves gives me chills—that grace, those reflexes. They say stackers have genetically diverged from humanity. Watching Maude, I believe it. "I got one of them," she says carelessly. "The other one, I dunno, have you seen him?"

She's killed Sam?!?

I flinch deeper into the Porsche's shadow. When Maude turns the other way, I crawl across the strip of sunlight between the Porsche and the next car. Crawl, crawl, rest in the shadow of a chemical-smelling undercarriage. Crawl, crawl, rest.

"I don't know where they are," Imogen says, with an edge of panic in her voice.

"Oh, because you're just a taxi driver. Riiiight." Maude pauses, her head cocked on one side. "Didn't you say you work for the Bratva?"

"Maybe not anymore," Imogen mumbles.

"That's a shame. If you did work for the Bratva, we'd be on the same side. Kind of."

"How come?"

"They're subcontractors for Big Tech. I am, too."

"I thought the XS Group was hired sales muscle," Imogen says, resisting the horrible truth that now unfolds itself within my mind.

"Well, yeah," Maude says. "And who do you think hire us? Big Tech. There isn't anyone else to work for in this fucking galaxy."

"There's Wall Street," Imogen says bleakly.

"Oh, sure. I did that for about five minutes. Then I went where the real money is."

Poor Ruby, and he thought that if he wanted to make real money, he had to join the pirates.

Maude paces, sweeping each side of the parking lot with her rifle. I can see the tension in her shoulders. Whatever it is in her that makes her snap, it's building.

"So the King invites us to his party," and I can hear her gritting her teeth as she talks, "which is like inviting yourself, but never mind. It's not a party, anyway."

"It's a trade show," Imogen whispers.

"Yep. The moveable feast of conspicuous consumption. Same faces, different planet every weekend. Ghost Train, whatever, there's always some excuse. Don't pity the one-percenters. They're there to be sold on the next big thing. Last year it was force fields. This year it's biomodding. OK, so it was the year of biomodding in 2061, and every five years before that, but now the market is finally taking off. So this should be Flower Lake's year, right? Right? And it totally would have been, if that little retard hadn't smashed a fucking display case. And it's all my fault, because *I* vetted them to go to the party. I played it safe, I only took *one* post-op freak, and he screws me over. Fucking classic."

Imogen speaks. Her voice is stronger. The flame of outrage has been lit. "Don't you think it's unethical for Big Tech to sanction this shit? I mean, people are playing with their lives here."

And Imogen doesn't know the half of it, I think, lying with my face pressed to the ground. She wasn't there when I got Ruby to tell me the truth about the surgery's failure rate.

I crawl on, flat on my belly. Only two cars to go to the Lamborghini, and I don't know what I'm going to do when I get there, but it will be violent.

Behind me, Imogen answers her own question. "It's extremely unethical, and it's also stupid. How much does the King make from patient fees? It's gotta be chump change."

"You're not thinking big enough," Maude says dryly. "This is a research project that will unlock the mysteries of Krell technology to create a better future for humanity. So, not stupid. Unethical, however? Yep. Absolutely. And that's why I'm going to kill you."

I freeze at these words. I can't see Imogen, but she must

have frozen, too, because the next thing I hear is Maude's laughter.

"You think I'm kidding, don't you?"

"I think there's a normal woman hiding behind the gun and the attitude," Imogen says in a brave, shaky voice. "I've met her. She was cool. She likes Broadway musicals and vintage fashion."

The Lamborghini's bumper pokes into the petals, bending them over. I didn't park it very well. I slide up over the bumper, brace my hands on the bonnet—

—and stare into a hole where the windscreen used to be.

All the windows are gone, the seats destroyed, memory-foam oozing out of rips in the leather upholstery. Maude's shot it to crap.

My mind races.

That means the bullets that hit the hotel—

—were fired by someone else.

Ah, Fletch, you idjit. Of course they were. That was a machine-gun firing at the hotel. Maude's rifle couldn't do that—well, technically it could, but I can't see her holding down the trigger in automatic mode and wildly spraying the hotel building. She's more of the one shot, one kill type.

I half-hear her and Imogen engaging in a brittle repartee. Imogen's finally succeeded in distracting Maude from her lethal mission, if only for a few moments. Careful to make as little noise as possible, I haul myself over the bonnet and slide through the Lamborghini's shattered windscreen. I land in a pile of safety glass fragments in the passenger seat. It's not sharp-edged, it just feels like gravel.

On the floor in the back, Sam lies in a pool of his own blood. He's only wearing his borrowed swimsuit, and he looks so defenceless and young that I have to chew my lips to stay in control.

I reach between the seats and pull my trousers out from under him. They're soaked with blood. Pieces of safety glass roll off his chest. They land on the floor amid glittering brass ...

... shell casings?

Fact o' God, I didn't even notice until now that there's a hatch open in the roof of the Lamborghini, and a belt of ammunition hanging down through it, glinting in the sunshine.

So that's what that queer box behind the back seats was.

It's now a mini Gatling gun sticking up through the roof between two half-moon shield panels.

The owners of Lamborghinis, after all, can afford to have them customized.

Right. We're in business now. Maude, not her real name, is going to regret the day she tangled with Baron Short of Pervée.

I start to crawl over Sam's body on my hands and knees. His blood is sticky on my bare legs. She'll fecking pay for this ...

Sam opens his eyes.

OH JESUS!

I swallow a shout of astonishment.

Sam struggles to sit up, grimacing, clamping one hand to the bullet wound in his neck that killed him, but didn't kill him, but should have killed him if this is still the same world I woke up in this morning. I hold him down, trying to communicate with my eyes alone that he's got to be quiet.

That's when I notice the Gizmo buried an inch deep in

his stomach.

I pull it out. It's not acquisitiveness, just instinct. When you see a five-inch nail stuck in somebody, you pull it out.

It leaves no puncture wound behind.

The Gizmo works. It fecking *works!* "Rejuvenation? More like resurrection," I breathe in disbelief. Although he can't actually have died, or he wouldn't have been able to stick it in himself.

That's how you're supposed to use it, according to the rumors. Just like an injection with a very big needle.

Sam reaches for the Gizmo—proving that his brush with death hasn't affected his wits *or* his agenda. I swiftly stick it down my Speedos.

What? I don't have anywhere else to put it.

I wedge it in there with the point facing *up,* believe me.

Rolling clear of Sam, I land in the far back. My underpants are lying on the floor. I take the Gizmo out and wrap it up in them, then return the whole bundle to its place—that feels a bit less perilous.

I'm on a turntable that'll allow the Gatling gun to rotate 360°. I poke my head up through the hatch in the roof and peek around one of the vertical shield panels

Imogen and Maude are standing in the middle of the parking lot, giving out to each other. It sounds like the finals of a victimhood tournament, each one loudly trying to make out that she is more to be pitied. I can't do anything until Imogen gets out of the way. I finger the ammo strip hanging over the side of the feed tray, hoping it's not jammed.

"Mom," Sam says at my feet. His voice is loud and slurred—he's not fully conscious, after all. "I'm coming.

Wait for me. Don't die, OK, Mom? Hold on until I get there."

"Shut the feck up!" I yelp, appalled.

But it's too late.

Maude spins around to face the Lamborghini.

I fumble in panic with the Gatling gun.

All in the same motion—those reflexes!—Maude drops her rifle and seizes Imogen in a chokehold. As if by magic her handgun appears. It's the same one she threatened us with in the taxi. Once again it's pressed against Imogen's head, and this time I have no doubt she will shoot.

CHAPTER 13

Maude grinds her gun against Imogen's head. "Get out of the car with your hands up!" she screams. "I'm gonna count to five, asshole! Five ... four ..."

If I do as she says she'll kill Imogen anyway, and me as well. I stand up, aim at the bus on the other side of the parking lot, and squeeze off a burst from the mini Gatling gun.

Jesus, this thing chews through the ammo! The belt's half gone by the time my finger comes off the trigger. Hot casings bounce off my bare shins.

Bullet holes decorate the bus but Maude hasn't moved an inch. Right. That didn't work.

"This swimsuit really isn't your color," she says to Imogen. Her voice is a treacly coo. It's worse than if she were still screaming. "A touch of red might improve it. And gray. I love the combination of red and gray."

Imogen starts to cry. How hard she tried to get through to Maude, and how completely useless it was. Welcome to my world, Ms. Kincaid.

A loud robotic voice says, "Enough of this bullshit," and

I jump out of my skin, because for a minute there it felt like time had stopped and nothing was ever going to happen again, apart from Imogen crying and me feeling helpless.

"Drop your gun and walk away from her," the same voice says. "Actually, drop both of your guns. And all the other weapons you've probably got hidden in that G.I. Jane outfit."

A small black sphere rises over the roof of the hotel. It's a high-end security drone. For a crazy minute I hope it belongs to Finian. Maybe a truck-mounted rocket launcher wasn't the only technology he brought along to extend his range.

But, no. On the side of the drone it says FLOWER LAKE HEALTH & BEAUTY RESORT.

The drone has a bloody great gun sticking out of the side of it.

It zips out over the parking lot and points its gun at Maude.

Maude frowns up at the drone. She's standing in the circular pool of shade it casts. Imogen backs away slowly. "Who's operating this thing?" Maude says to the drone.

"The trouble with being a stacker," says the drone, "is that your automatic assumption of superiority can sometimes lead you astray."

It's *Ruby* operating the drone! Good old Ruby!

"Oh, you must be that ex-stacker who just got hired in the custodial division," Maude says. "Yeah, actually, I did make a note of you. And guess what? You're fired."

She raises her rifle and opens up on the drone.

"Imogen!" I shout. "Over here!"

Her head jerks around. She dashes between the parked

cars. Maude whirls. I pull the trigger of the Gatling gun again. The noise is frightful, a buzzing bass drone that eats my ears from the inside. I destroy the bodywork of several cars but I don't hit Maude. She runs across the parking lot, pursued by the drone. Pieces of cactus gout up at her heels. Ruby's aim is terrible, too. Or more likely, he's just not used to operating the drone. He must have sneaked into the security office when he realized what was going on. He's sacrificed his job and quite possibly his freedom to save our lives. I take back every insulting thing I've ever thought or said about him.

Imogen dives through the windcsreen into the driver's seat of the Lamborghini. She feverishly brushes glass onto the floor and starts the engine. I'm trying to feed another belt of ammo into the mini Gatling. All this technology we're not used to. It doesn't even have to be A-tech to have a bloody steep learning curve. When I have my own planet there'll be no tech on it at all, apart from my spaceship and my television. Imogen's still got the Krell artefact stuck in her hair.

The Lamborghini rises into the air. As soon as we clear the perimeter fence, Imogen guns the rocket engine and we scream off over the lake.

With all its windows gone, the Lamborghini is effectively a convertible. A torrent of air pummels us. I have to turn my face sideways to breathe without choking. Imogen squints her eyes nearly closed. "Back to the spaceport?" she shrieks over the wind.

"Yes!" I yell back.

I suppose we're both thinking the same thing: Finian now looks like the lesser of two evils.

I glance back down at Flower Lake … and my heart sinks. Maude's car is rising from the parking lot. The drone chases it for a short distance and then falls back.

On the floor in the back, Sam sits up. He pulls himself onto the back seat. Awareness clicks into his eyes like the numbers lining up in a combination lock.

"Come here and show me how to feed this belt into the gun," I roar, knowing that he managed to do it before, to the extent of nearly emptying the ammo crate.

"Uhhh? What? Oh. The gun. OK."

He scrambles between the seats, dappled with dried blood, but fully healed. The funny thing is he looks thinner. His cheekbones and hip bones stick out as if he's been starving. I suppose the Gizmo must have got the energy to heal his wounds from somewhere.

"You just hook it onto here, yes? Then you flip this lever." He's happy; he's been handling firearms all his life. He edges me off the turntable and rotates it to point the gun backwards. Hunched over the sights, he yells, "Come on, baby!"

"I didn't know your mother was ill, Sam."

He tenses up. "She isn't."

"Then why are you afraid she's going to die? They treat them fairly well in prison." At least I hope they do, because that's where we're going.

"So I hear, man, so I hear." He doesn't look at me. "But she's eighty-fucking-two. She gave birth to me when she was in her fifties. Yeah, telomerase repair and all that jazz … but eighty-two is still old, and people tend to die when they get old. Especially if they've recently lost a war and been shipped back to Earth under military guard."

I watch Maude's car rise up through the air. "So you were going to steal the Gizmo and take it to her?"

He nods.

"Into a maximum security jail? Past the layers of guards and body scanners and feck knows what?"

"I'd have figured it out, man. I always figure something out."

And his breath hitches in his chest. He turns his head away, but I can see wetness glistening on his eyelashes in the light of Arnold's long evening.

"You're all right," I tell him. I should hug him, but I'm Irish. I touch his arm awkwardly. "You're all right, Sam."

"I'm sorry, man. You guys have been friends to me. This last year? Working construction? We had a good time. Yeah, the work was shit, but we had a good time, didn't we?"

"We did."

Maybe they still offer rock-breaking as a recreational activity in modern prisons.

"But I just felt like I had to go through with it."

"Sam." I have to ask. "Did you try to crash the car into me and Imogen on purpose?"

"Huh?"

"In the scrapyard."

He jerks around to face me, eyes wide. "No, man! The car was out of control. Did you think I was trying to hit you?"

"It occurred to me."

"Fletch, if I wanted you dead, you would be dead." Sam's not boasting. His voice is flat. "I *don't* want you dead. I just wanted the Gizmo, for my mom. So … OK. Back at the hotel, I put a few bullets into the door to keep you inside, so I could get away with the Gizmo. But I was *not* trying to kill you."

It would be easy to disbelieve him. Believing him is harder. But it is the right thing to do. "All right, Sam. I'm sorry. I had to ask."

"*I'm* sorry," he says. "I screwed up big-time."

"No use crying over spilt milk," I say.

Maude's car is catching up. The tinted windscreen catches the sun. We're flying over the frilly waves of cactus petals now, high above the usual lanes of traffic.

Sam hunches over the gun. "Come on, you fucking bitch!" he screams. "Come and get it!"

I pry him away from the gun, gently but firmly. "Sam, she's not got any armaments on that. It's just a company car."

"How do you know?"

"Because she'd have shot us out of the sky by now if she did. Anyway, she's not after the Gizmo."

"Huh?" he says, unable to understand how anyone could *not* be after the Gizmo.

"Not everyone in the galaxy is interested in A-tech. She's just doing her job. Suppressing bad publicity for her employers."

"That's one hell of a job."

"It is."

Maude's car slowly but steadily overhauls us. The driver's side window cracks open. A gloved hand comes out with a gun in it, and shoots at us. Sam and I duck.

"Imogen! Can this jalopy go any faster?"

It can.

Our journey back to the spaceport is a blur of speed, noise, and wind. High above the maze city, Maude brings her car alongside us and sideswipes us. She's figured out we aren't going to shoot her. So we do shoot her—her car, that is. Sam places a burst neatly in her engine compartment. That kills her rocket engine, so now she's flying on momentum and anti-grav alone.

We pull ahead, until the Lamborghini runs out of fuel.

This happens when we're just a mile or two from the spaceport. "I can make an unpowered landing," Imogen says. She no longer has to shout over the wind, as we're losing speed rapidly.

"Do it."

We sink towards the factories and depots around the spaceport.

Behind us, Maude's car drifts down on the same glide path.

"We're going to overshoot the parking lot!" Imogen says. "I'll have to land in the launch zone!"

"Ah, feck."

We glide over the visitor parking lot. It seems as if we're still going terrifyingly fast. The sun is setting beyond the spaceport, turning Arnold's thin atmosphere orange on the horizon. We squeak over the terminal building, so low the wheels clip an antenna sticking up from the roof, and hurtle towards the ground.

They haven't bothered to asphalt the launch zone. It's bare desert. The wheels touch, bounce, touch. Dust sprays up. We roll to a halt, half a mile from the terminal building.

The squeal and crunch of metal pulls my gaze around.

Maude didn't make it over the terminal building! She's landed on the roof, tearing a swathe through the forest of antennas and satellite dishes up there.

I wonder for a second if some part of her *wants* to lose her job. Or maybe even wants to die. The suicide rate for stackers is quite high. .

Suicidal adventures are not out of reach for the rest of us, however.

I climb out of the Lamborghini's windscreen. The doors aren't working since Maude sideswiped us.

The terminal's sweep of windows frame a reflection of the sunset. Between us and the building stands a sleek, porpoise-shaped private spaceship whose matte black paint job swallows the light.

Two NEPD vehicles stand a short distance away—a patrol cruiser and a cargo ship. I suppose that's how they got the rocket launcher here.

A clump of people stare in our direction, frozen in cringing poses.

All except Finian, whom I recognize by his mustache as well as his uniform. He's neither cringing nor frozen. He stumps towards the Lamborghini, carrying something—I expect it's a weapon—in his right hand.

Imogen and Sam get out.

"Well, I guess this is it," Sam says. "It was nice knowing you guys."

CHAPTER 14

Sam, Imogen and I stand in a line, watching Finian plod towards us. Our shadows stretch towards the spaceport terminal, long and skinny, like the shadows of aliens.

"I hope there aren't any TV cameras," Sam mutters. "It would be kind of embarrassing to make the evening news wearing a swimsuit and a sunburn."

"I just wanted a normal life," Imogen says.

"You're not alone, darlin'," I say, although my own dream of owning a planet is not what you'd call a normal life. Or maybe it is. Maybe you have to get thousands of lightyears from the rest of humanity to have a normal life these days.

Imogen looks up at me. The low-angled light flatters her sunburnt complexion. Her hair's a rat's nest of tangles and Krell wires and crystals, she's wearing a borrowed swimsuit with a dirty shirt over it, and she's never looked lovelier. "I have to ask you something, Fletch."

"Go ahead." With half of my attention, I watch Finian walk towards us. He's got a fair distance to cover and he's in no hurry. One of the other people is coming after him now.

"Why did you introduce me as your fiancée?"

That grabs 100% of my attention. I gaze down at her, drinking in her beauty like a condemned man enjoying his last drink. "The truth is I'm in love with you. Sure I'm an idjit. All I've ever done is get you into trouble."

Her eyes go wide and soft. Then she recovers and says tartly, "I'm perfectly capable of getting into trouble on my own, buster."

It may be my last chance ever, so I bend down and kiss her. There's not time for it to be more than a peck on the lips. I can't tell if she's kissing me back. At least she doesn't pull away. Sam hoots salaciously.

I straighten up and there's Finian glowering at us. The sunset's shining in his eyes, so he has to squint. It's not a gun he's carrying, it's a Starbucks cup, but the gun is there at his hip.

"Are you turning yourself in?" His voice drops for an instant. "I'm disappointed in you, lad."

Then the flash of the old Finian is gone. The other fella catches up to him: a tall fella in a Nintendo t-shirt and jeans.

Finian clears his throat and booms at us: "Hands in the air, miscreants!"

Where are his minions? Oh, there they are, descending towards the roof of the terminal building in a police flitter. I wonder if Maude will get arrested, too.

I suspect not. Because I recognize the man in the Nintendo t-shirt, and knowing what I now know, the odds are he's Maude's employer.

"That's my car," he says. "I *knew* I ordered a Lamborghini. Huh, looks like they did a nice job with the customization. Where'd you find it?" This to me.

"In a scrap yard," I say.

"Figures. Bunch of crooks on this moon."

"And most of them work for you," I say. "What's the world coming to when a man's own employees steal his car?"

The man frowns. "Who are you, anyway?"

I have had enough of the Baron Short charade. "The name's Fletcher Connolly."

The man looks from me, to Finian—who has a nametag that says CONNOLLY below his sheriff's star—and back again.

"My nephew," Finian says, flatly. "He's so dense he's got his own fecking event horizon."

Sam sniggers. "And I thought *I* had problems with my family."

"That's Sam Haddad," Finian goes on. "The girl is Imogen Kincaid, a former Samsung employee."

The mention of Samsung makes the man in the Nintendo t-shirt smile. His name is Matthew Steiner and he's a co-founder of Moto, one of Samsung's competitors. The Nintendo t-shirt is an ironic reference to one of the companies Moto crushed with its immersive gaming experiences. They still call Moto a startup but it's the biggest of the new A-tech exploitation companies challenging the Big Tech rulers of the roost. Matthew Steiner has his own tree on Treetop—and I suspect he has extensive holdings on Arnold, as well.

Of course he's a stacker.

"Nice to meet you, too," I say. I'm confronting a centibillionaire wearing nothing but a pair of Speedos. My life is complete. Lord, now let thy servant go in peace.

And, of course, Imogen is also wearing a swimsuit, and

has an A-tech artefact on her head.

"I need that back," Matthew Steiner says, pointing at the Krell artefact. "The King is kind of attached to it."

"And what've you got to do with the King?" I say rudely.

Sam's helping Imogen untangle the artefact from her hair.

"He's a friend," Steiner says.

"Bullshit," Imogen says. "He's Moto's biggest individual shareholder."

I hear an echo of Maude's voice: *There's no one else to work for in this galaxy…* I glance at the terminal building. The police flitter has landed at the edge of the roof. One officer stands on its wing.

"So the King uses you to do his dirty work, huh?" Imogen says.

Steiner doesn't like that. "The artefact," he says crisply, holding out his hand. He expects us to walk over and give it to him.

Sam meets my gaze, his eyebrows raised. I take the Krell artefact from him. Steiner's eyes track it.

"We were told by a source within your organization, Mr. Steiner, that this is just a toy," I say, extrapolating from Maude's contempt for the object. "But I don't think it is, is it?"

"It's being researched," he says. "If the research can't proceed, we'll never know." He speaks as if *never knowing* is the worst fate in the world.

"Ah yes," I say. "The research. Would that be the research into the physiology of the Krell race, which is being undertaken at a location near here, with the assistance of aspiring biomodders?"

Steiner starts to speak. I hold up the Krell artefact and

give it a good twist. One of the fragile wires breaks with a *snap*. Steiner closes his mouth.

"People have died to assist you with your research, Mr. Steiner. Their bodies have been thrown out with the rubbish. Yes, I know you're about to say they signed disclaimers and waivers and all that shite. They accepted ten thousand pages of terms and conditions without reading them, and that puts you in the clear, I suppose."

Finian slurps from his Starbucks cup, his eyes hooded. His silence is all the encouragement I need to go on. I'm shivering in my near-nakedness as the sun goes down, and I'm as angry as I have ever been in my life.

"It's a sickness in my opinion, Mr. Steiner. And I'm not exempting myself. We're starting to think A-tech can solve all the troubles of the universe. It's like a religion, actually. And you're very good at selling it to consumers."

Steiner actually smiles at what he takes for a tribute to his achievements.

"But your business is heading for the rocks, isn't it? Because we're finding out that there are limits. All the low-hanging fruit has been picked. It's getting harder and harder to reverse-engineer A-tech discoveries, because we do not understand the thought processes of the aliens who made the stuff. You're very intelligent, I have no doubt, but you don't understand how they thought, either." I shake the Krell artefact. A crystal falls off. Steiner spasms. "Take the Krells. They were particularly inscrutable. The King's had this item in his collection for ages, and you don't even know if it was a toy, or an advanced aqualung, or the key to the seventh seal of the apocalypse."

"Hence this research project," Steiner says with forced

calm.

"Yes, this bloody evil research project! Operate on human beings so they look like Krells, and maybe they'll *become* Krells, and we'll finally find out what was in their heads! Build them and it will come, is that the idea? It's nothing but a fecking cargo cult."

I'm not really angry at him. I'm angry at myself. Have I not worshipped at that same altar, forsaking all else to pursue A-tech, because I want to ascend to alien status myself: Fletch, planetary overlord?

"Jesus, we're primitives," I choke out.

Steiner's hot to defend his project. "DNA does actually affect neurological function," he says.

Imogen lets out a cry of disgust. It takes me another minute to realize what Steiner just said. It's not just surgery. They're implanting alien DNA into human beings—and that's probably why this artefact matters so much to them! It's got loads of DNA on it from long-dead Krells using it as a snorkel.

Click. Finian unfolds his arms and opens one of his enormous fists. A rubberized cylinder expands into a whippy baton. "Thank you, Mr. Steiner, for confirming that you are conducting illegal genetic engineering experiments," he says. "Your confession has been recorded and transmitted to a secure server. You have the right to remain silent …"

Steiner stares at him like the desert itself rose up and spoke with a human voice. "You're supposed to arrest *them.* Do your fucking job."

"My job is to uphold the law," Finian says. "Which you just admitted to breaking."

"Talk to my lawyers," Steiner says without missing a beat. "And give me that fucking artefact."

I pretend to ponder it for a moment. Then I pass the Krell artefact to Imogen. She crushes it in her bare hands, twisting the wires until they snap, and drops it to the ground. I step on it, grinding it into the dust. The little crystals disintegrate under my heel. It's so old.

A little voice in my head wails that I'm destroying millions of dollars. But there's a heady satisfaction to the deed. The look of dumbfounded horror on Steiner's face makes it all the sweeter.

Even Finian stares in astonishment. Knowing my history, he must think I've lost my wits. Me—destroying A-tech?

Of course he's got no idea that I have another A-tech artefact, worth a hundred times more, stuffed down my Speedos.

Steiner makes a convulsive movement towards us. Finian lowers his baton to block his way. The A-tech mogul spins on his heel. "Happy now?" he barks at Finian. "You fucking Luddite."

"Insulting the badge won't get you anywhere, Mr. Steiner." Finian takes a pair of handcuffs of his belt. "It'll be best for yourself if you come quietly."

Steiner steps back. Hands on his hips, he sneers at the aged Irish sheriff with his funny accent and his white moustache. I wonder if he has any idea who Finian used to be. "You clearly didn't get the memo," he says. "The NEPD was created to enforce law and order."

He goes on lecturing Finian about how law and order is defined by what Big Tech wants, and while he's distracted, I reach in through the passenger side window of the

Lamborghini and pluck my lightsaber out of the mug holder. I picked up a spare powerpack for it from the amenities tray at the Flower Lake Health & Beauty Resort. I meet Sam's eyes.

There are two perfectly good spaceships over there. The only thing we don't know is which, if either, of them has a stacker on board. No stackee, no flyee—we can't go interstellar without a stacker.

But there's a stacker right here, blathering at Finian about shortsighted Luddites who impede technological progress.

"We'll take him prisoner," I breathe to Sam, who nods enthusiastically. It would be very satisfying indeed to make Matthew Steiner operate our getaway ship.

At that moment Finian cuts Steiner off by taking his radio from his belt and speaking into it. "Unit One, come in."

The radio hisses.

Finian glances up at the terminal building. He's waiting for his backup to appear. We'd better leg it before they arrive.

At the moment, however, I can see no signs of life up there. The sun is still shining on the roof, and the police flitter stands motionless.

"Unit One, come in," Finian repeats.

The police flitter lifts off the roof. But Finian's radio is still silent.

Imogen whispers, "Look at Steiner."

My blood runs cold. He's smiling.

"Run!" I shout. *"Run!"*

CHAPTER 15

Imogen and Sam sprint across the launch zone.

I pounce at Steiner, intending to take him hostage. It's now or never. I thumb-press the button of my lightsaber, and the blue beam leaps out, as thick as a child's wrist, glowing eerily in the twilight.

Steiner recoils—

—straight into Finian's arms.

"Got you now," Finian says, dragging Steiner's wrists behind his back and snapping the handcuffs on him.

Damn it.

My lightsaber sears the desert at their feet. The smell of burnt dust rises.

"As for you," Finian says to me, "put that weapon away, and put some fecking clothes on. You can tell me later what you're doing here, when everyone thought you were dossing on Arcadia."

The police flitter skims closer, pale and sinister against the darkening sky. Steiner's not struggling anymore. He watches the flitter, smiling.

"Run, Finian!" I yell. "That's not your officers in there!

It's Maude!"

"Who's Maude?"

"Ah, it's not her real name. Just run!"

Finian jerks Steiner towards him by the short bar joining the handcuffs. He stands him in front of him like a human shield, which is a good precaution. Unfortunately there's only one Steiner to go around.

I take my own advice and run.

Imogen and Sam are far ahead, running in opposite directions. Their bare legs flash in the twilight. Imogen appears to be making for the patrol cruiser, while Sam has his eye on Matthew Steiner's streamlined private spaceship. Fecking typical.

The police flitter glides towards them. It stalls in the air, as if Maude can't decide which of them to strafe first. Then she veers towards Imogen, and lightning flashes out from the flitter's nose cannon.

Imogen crumples to the ground.

I thought I was already running flat out. I discover that I can run faster.

I'm still a hundred yards from Imogen's body when the flitter swoops towards me like a bird of prey.

Several thoughts dart through my mind:

1. The NEPD aren't allowed to use lethal force.
2. Finian has probably refitted this flitter to get around that annoying little restriction.
3. You can increase the voltage of an electropulse laser to make it lethal, but you can't increase its effective range.
4. My lightsaber has a range of 30 meters.

I stop running and brace my legs apart. I remember

Imogen in the scrap yard. *Wait … wait … wait …*

Now!

I stab up at the oncoming flitter, holding the lightsaber steady, so that the beam saws a smoking gouge down the underside of the fuselage.

The nose cannon flashes.

I dive sideways, rolling away. An unknown number of volts crack into the desert behind me, ionizing the dust.

I pick myself up and sprint onwards.

Sam's already reached Imogen. He's stooping over her, trying to lift her, as I pant up. "She's OK!" he says. "It was a stun charge!"

Well, well. Finian did not refit his flitter, after all. Maybe he couldn't get away with it.

A wave of relief washes over me, loosening my muscles. I shoulder Sam out of the way and pick Imogen up. I pass my lightsaber to Sam, as I no longer have a free hand for it.

"The Gulfstream," he says.

"No, the patrol cruiser," I say.

"It's not Railroad-capable!"

"And it's not got biometric locks and feck knows what, either. It would be a different story if we had the treecats with us. As it is, we're limited to what we can steal."

Behind us, the police flitter crashes.

It's not a very spectacular crash. No flames, no wreckage. The flitter just ploughs its nose into the desert and tips to one side. I suppose I must have hit the drive control train, or something like that.

Maude jumps out of the cockpit, a camouflage-colored blur of energy. It's quiet enough I hear her screaming at Finian to let Steiner go.

The steps of the patrol cruiser are already down. Sam vanishes up them like a squirrel into a tree. I stumble behind him with Imogen in my arms. Jesus, she could stand to lose a little weight. But she's breathing, she's breathing. I mount the stairs and lay her down on the deck inside.

There are two seats up front, jumpseats on the walls in the back. Sam's got the cockpit light on. The dashboard controls blink a welcome. There is no one to stop us. They're all lying dead on the roof of the terminal.

Except Finian.

"Give me my lightsaber," I say, grabbing it off the copilot's seat. "I'll be straight back."

I jog back across the desert, knowing this is one of the stupidest things I've ever done, in a life bursting at the seams with stupidity.

As it turns out, I don't have to go very far. Finian's dragging Steiner towards the ships, while Maude prowls at their heels. She's gesturing with her handgun, which seems out of character. She must be very upset. Aiding my brilliant deduction, she's screaming about how she will tell the King everything.

Finian gets a word in sideways. "The King *knows* everything. That's why I was ordered to destroy the artefact and the thieves who had it, as well as anyone who abetted their escape."

Maude's gun hand drops. She's genuinely shocked. "You were ordered to kill *me?* I was trying to fix the situation."

Finian lets go of Steiner, wipes his brow. "He didn't mention your name, love."

Maude rounds on Steiner. *"You* gave the orders!"

"I did not order the destruction of the artefact!" Steiner

shouts. Arrogant, even in handcuffs. "This crazy old cop is out of control!"

"Well, the rocket launcher was provided to us by the King himself," Finian says. "Sometimes we all need to take a step back and realize that we ourselves, and our most cherished dreams, are just numbers on a spreadsheet to the real masters of the universe."

What is society coming to when Finian Connolly sounds like the sanest person on the scene?

"The King cut his losses," Finian says. "It's as simple as that."

But Maude is no longer listening.

With a scream of rage, she raises her gun and shoots Steiner in the face.

Pop, pop, pop.

The reports echo across the desert, and Steiner falls.

I put on a desperate burst of speed. I have to reach Maude before she adds Finian to her kill tally. I jam my thumb on the button—

But Maude's not shooting anymore. She falls to her knees, hands over her face, doubling up on the ground.

Finian pounces.

And my lightsaber ends up cleaving the air between them, a bright barrier. Finian freezes, inches from walking into the beam.

"Step back, Uncle," I say. "Don't hurt her. She's hurt enough already. Leave her alone."

Walking closer, I pick Maude's gun up from where she dropped it.

CHAPTER 16

I get Finian into the police cruiser with Maude's gun at his back. It's a Glock, half the magazine remaining.

"Sit down and shut up, Uncle."

I may not have wanted to see him murdered, but I'm perfectly happy to see him tied into a jump seat, glowering in impotent fury.

"Hurry up and take off, Sam."

"I've never actually done a launch to orbit," Sam says, from the cockpit. "Isn't Imogen awake yet?"

"She is not." I've laid her on the floor with a bulletproof vest for a pillow. I check her pulse and lay the back of my hand on her forehead, keeping an eye on Finian all the time. "Even when she wakes up, she's not going to be in any shape. You can do it."

"I'll do it," Finian offers.

"I said shut up. Sam?"

"Don't blame me when we end up splattered across a thousand square miles of Arnold," he says glumly, and executes a perfect launch to orbit.

I hold my breath until the dashboard tells us we've

escaped from the moon's gravity well. Then I give Sam a high five. "Nice work, Bond."

"Now I know what it really feels like to be an immortal alien. It's not that much fun." He grins tiredly and unbuckles. On the long-range viewscreen, Arnold shrinks to a mottled green crescent. Goodbye to another horrible corner of the galaxy I'll never visit again.

"Seven hours to Treetop," I say.

"More like six. This baby is faster than the taxi. I've locked in the autopilot." Sam steps out from between the front seats, leaving the cockpit vacant. I take his place, just because it seems as if there should be someone in the driver's seat. "Is there any food on board?" Sam says hopefully. "Donuts?" He grins at Finian, who ignores him.

Searching the lockers in the back, Sam whoops. "Quinoa bagels, snack packs of hummus and baby carrots, trail mix … and coconut water. Figures; this is the *Treetop* precinct."

He proceeds to eat his way through the patrol's entire emergency food stash.. I grab a bagel for myself before they're all gone, and watch him enthusiastically chewing. I'm struck again by how thin he looks. No wonder he's hungry.

The Gizmo digs into my lower stomach. I touch it, remembering how it healed Sam. It's the spookiest piece of A-tech I've ever handled. And it's got to be worth even more than we expected.

Finian sees me apparently touching myself. "Did you have surgery yourself at that place?" he says. "Sure that's a champion bulge."

"Feck off with you," I say.

"Either that or you've got a sock in your underpants."

"Swimming togs."

"You're going to be the laughing-stock of the galaxy when you do the perp walk in that costume."

I resolve to ignore him. "Sam?" He's sitting in the back amidst a litter of food wrappers, alternately belching and yawning. "We need to work out what we're going to do when we reach Treetop."

"Yeah, man. We land in some out-of-the-way location. Ditch the cruiser. Hook up with Donal and Harriet. Use their connections in the catering industry to get a ride back to Arcadia. Once we get there, we'll have options."

This is the kind of plan the son of Special Delivery Sam *would* come up with. I've already rejected it, and many variants of it, because I refuse to put Donal and Harriet in danger. Also, I want to deal with the Russians from a distance of several hundred lightyears. Anything less would be hazardous to our health.

I'm toying with a plan for resurrecting our aristocratic identities to get onto a commercial flight to Earth. As I'm about to start explaining this, Sam yawns again, hugely.

"Fletch, I'm done in. I have to grab some sleep, or I'll be a wreck when we get there. Dunno why I'm so tired," he says, childishly, and curls up on the floor next to Imogen. He's asleep the second his head hits the deck. Watching the two of them lie there, I feel an overwhelming surge of protectiveness.

The cruiser roars on through deep space. I switch off the cockpit light to let Sam and Imogen sleep. The quiet goes on and on. I fight drowsiness, and lose the fight. When my head jerks up, five and a half hours have gone past.

I think Finian's asleep, too, but then I see his eyes gleam in the dark.

"You'll never get away with it," he says.

"Oh yes we will," I say. "We're in a *police cruiser*. And you'll tell us all the right things to say when they come on the radio."

"The feck I will. Jail is the only place you're going."

I feel a mild pang of desperation. I don't know what to say. What comes out is, "Please …"

"I'm disappointed in you." He said that before. "I don't blame the lad there. With the upbringing he had, it's no wonder. But you were raised better than this. Your parents will say it's my fault for leading you astray, and no doubt they'll be right to a certain extent. But you've got a brain on you. Why use it for this?"

Again, I don't know what to say. I turn away from him and go through the motions of reviewing the readouts on the dashboard. We're only a few thousand miles from Treetop now. The planet's green orb fills the windscreen.

Arnold has shrunk to moon-size on the long-range viewscreen. In my memory, Maude is frozen in time, curled up in a fetal position in the launch zone, crying for everything she's done. Realistically, someone's probably put her out of her misery by now.

"You're a queer one, Fletch," Finian rumbles. Amusement glints in his eyes. "You won't work for a living, but it must have been enough work getting into that party."

He knows we were at the party. Of course, he thinks we stole the Krell artefact from there. Does he know about the Gizmo, too? He can't.

"Sure it looked desperate dull. You'd have had better craic at the local pub."

He has his mind made up that I'm a chronic skiver. I

consider telling him that I've spent the last year working construction, breaking my back like a Paddy across the water a hundred years ago, which is more than he's ever done. But the whole point of that was so I'd never have to do it again. So he's right. He's right about the party, too, but I will not give him the satisfaction of saying so.

"Agh," my uncle grunts, having failed to bait me. "I've got to use the jacks."

"You can hold on."

"I'm about to piss myself. You know at my age, my bladder control isn't what it used to be."

I scowl. "All right."

I undo the bungee cords I used to strap him into the jumpseat. I'd also put some plastic handcuffs on him.

"I can't undo my flies with these on," he says, holding up his cuffed hands.

"You can, sure."

"No, I can't. Would you help me?" Grin, grin under his moustache. He's enjoying this. He looms over me in the dimness of the back. I'm 6'1" in my sock feet but he's a shade taller even than that. It is very difficult for me to stand my ground, even though I've got my lightsaber in my hand. He's had the whip hand over me all my life—the role reversal is jarring.

"Fine," I say, and release the plastic handcuffs with the little key.

He goes into the closet-sized loo at the back. The door locks.

I stand outside with my lightsaber in my hand.

Imogen stirs.

"Fletch?" Her voice is weak.

"How are you feeling, love?" I spare her a glance.

"Alive," she says, testing out her limbs. "I wasn't expecting that."

"Maude tased you."

"That, I got."

She stands up shakily, holding onto the overhead webbing. I want to go to her, but I daren't leave the bogs unguarded. "Finian's in the toilet," I say. "Could you go forward and have a look at the radar?"

"Are you kidding?"

"I am not. We're nearly there. If we can land at the north pole, that's what I want to do, but it depends on the traffic in orbit, the satellite coverage …"

"No, no, I mean *Finian* is *here?* On board? In the restroom at this moment?"

"He is."

She gives me a searching look. "You're either a better man than I thought you were, Fletcher Connolly," she says, "or a much worse one." With these enigmatic words she makes her way forward, stepping over the slumbering Sam and picking up a bottle of coconut water on the way.

I rattle the loo door. "Finian, have you had a heart attack in there?" My heart sinks; I may have guessed his strategy. He'll stay locked in there so we can't make him do the radio protocol for us. Then they'll know we're not really the police, and they'll shoot us down.

"Oh crap," Imogen says wearily.

"What?"

She's in the driver's seat. "The fucking Ghost Train's still here."

"How is that possible? We've been away …" It feels like a

lifetime. But when I add it up, it comes out to— "A bit less than twenty-three hours." And the Ghost Train halts for 27 hours, 3 minutes, and 40 seconds precisely, every time it visits Treetop or one of its other stops. "All right, so it's still here. Is that a problem?"

"It'll just make us more conspicuous. No one can use the Railroad until the Ghost Train's gone, so we'll be the only ship de-orbiting. *And* I'll have to fly right over the Railroad to enter a polar orbit. We'll be passing pretty close to the Ghost Train itself."

"Well, hopefully everyone's got bored and turned off their telescopes and cameras by now."

While I am uttering these fatuously optimistic words, the door of the loo bursts open, catching me in the shoulder, and Finian bursts out, brandishing a knife in an overhand grip.

He's better at hiding weapons than I am at finding them, obviously.

"You're under arrest, all of youse!" he bellows, his eyes flaming, daring me to try and take the knife off him.

It's only a measly little pocket-knife.

I daren't use my lightsaber in this enclosed space. The risk of killing someone, or piercing the hull, is too great.

So the instant Imogen screams, pulling Finian's gaze away, I charge him with my head down. I grab his wrist and head-butt him in the solar plexus.

We wrangle back and forth across the cabin, and step on Sam, who wakes up with a panicked shout.

I trip.

And somehow, I don't know how, the knife goes flying out of Finian's hand, passes an inch above Imogen's head, and sticks in the windscreen.

It's a *metalforma* knife.

Metalforma can cut through anything.

Even rad-hardened, impact-resistant, triple-layer spaceship window glass.

Having done its damage, the knife falls out of the windscreen, leaving a silver crack across the face of Treetop. I hear the thin shriek of escaping air.

There goes my last shred of optimism.

CHAPTER 17

Air whistles out through the hairline crack in the windscreen. Imogen's hair flies out horizontally. An empty tub of hummus hits me in the face, and that gives me an idea. I struggle out of Finian's slack grasp and scramble into the passenger seat. I left the blanket I was using to keep warm stuffed down the side of the seat. I slap it over the windscreen.

Mercifully, the shriek of escaping air falls silent.

The blanket covers half the windscreen, gradually getting sucked into the crack

"I can't see," Imogen screams.

She doesn't need to see out of the windscreen. She's got the instruments. I slide onto the floor and dig around in the litter, searching for Finian's knife. I heard it fall. Christ, it's a mess down here. Cops are almost as bad as taxi drivers.

"You're under arrest, Ms. Kincaid," Finian snarls. "Surrender control of this cruiser immediately, by order of the NEPD."

He's leaning between the seats, waving his badge in Imogen's face. I wonder if the NEPD really know what they've got here? Giving a sheriff's badge to a man like this is asking for wrongful death lawsuits.

He's cold-cocked Sam and all.

My hand closes on the hilt of his knife. Not the blade, thankfully. I hold it up, keeping it out of his reach. "Is this NEPD issue, Finian?"

I know it's not. Metalforma is illegal on Earth, for good reason. I shove it into an unneeded part of the dashboard.

"We'll drop you off along the way," I tell him. Maybe in deep space. The NEPD can thank me later.

Never one to back down when threatened, my uncle sneers, "All that effort, just for a shite wee Krell artefact that you broke to pieces, anyway."

I'm sick of his patronizing attitude. Recklessly, I pull the Gizmo out of my Speedos. It's a relief not to have it digging into me anymore. I unwrap it from my underpants and hold it up. "Nope, Uncle. All that effort was for this."

"Jesus fuck, is that what I think it is?" Finian exclaims.

Sam stirs. Blood glistens at the corner of his mouth. "Lemme see," he croaks.

Leaning back against the dashboard, I hold the Gizmo out of reach of grabby hands. I glance out the window on my side, which is oriented towards Treetop. The surface of the planet looks like a round ceiling. Tree canopies are dark green rosettes, as if the whole planet were done in plaster and painted green. There are several vehicles rising into orbit. They're probably responding to our arrival. And we've got to fly all the way to the north pole, and land without being noticed.

"We're screwed," Imogen weeps.

It is looking a bit that way.

I hold up the Gizmo. If we're about to be captured, I may as well get a good gloat in first. "You never found anything this valuable, did you, Finian? I'll tell you why. You weren't looking in the right places. Alien planets! The far reaches of the Railroad!" I make a rude noise. "The exploration industry's a game for losers, Finian. It's rigged against the little guy. We made *two* of the best finds of the last decade and we ended up as skint as ever. So I finally figured out the right place to look: in the reverse-R&D lab of a trillionaire's holiday house."

Finian stares at me, jaw sagging.

Did I say anything *that* shocking?

Imogen's sobbing, stamping on the pedals, swinging the yoke all over the place.

Actually, it is possible that Finian is not staring at me, but at something behind me.

I turn around to look out the windshield.

Well, that *is* quite a view.

We're about to deorbit past the local loop of the Railroad. Every habitable planet has a loop around it at an altitude of 9,000 miles, give or take, and we're coming up on that now. Since we've got no chain dogs on this cruiser, nothing to clamp on with, the Railroad will literally be immaterial to us; we'll just sail past it. But it *looks* like a rope across the universe, one of those A-tech ones they hang at the entrance of nightclubs, that give you a shock if you touch them. This far and no further, dirtwad.

And on that glimmering double arc, directly ahead of us, sits the Ghost Train.

We call our Railroad-capable vehicles ships, because that's what they are. Spaceships, equipped with nuclear thermal drives, for getting into orbit and down again.

But the Ghost Train never leaves the Railroad, so I suppose it doesn't need a conventional drive, although what do I know? What does anyone know about it? Only that it looks like an old-fashioned steam locomotive, pulling a string of capsule-style carriages joined by concertina locks, as if convergent evolution applied to machines as well as carbon-based species, which it does in the broad sense, for didn't every alien empire go through a sticks-and-stones age, then an industrial age, then an information age, and finally a space age, before smearing itself across the windscreen of the galaxy?

So maybe it's no great wonder that one of these civilizations built a train which can not only make a circuit of the galaxy every two years for umpty million years, but possesses an ability our ships do not, which is the power, once on the Railroad, to *stop*.

"I wish the bloody thing would hurry up and leave," I say uneasily.

"It's waiting for us!" Imogen sobs. "It thinks we're getting on board!"

"Well, it's wrong, isn't it? Go that way, we're going to pass too close to it."

Imogen jiggles the cruiser's controls in a panic.

"Everything's dead! It's not responding!"

"It's sucking us in," Sam says brokenly. "My mom knew a guy this happened to." He's crying. "I don't want to die!"

The Railroad fills the sky. The Ghost Train looms overhead, the size of several oil tankers joined end to end. We're drifting towards the boxcar, well, the bit on the end, anyway. I stare at the fractal steel tangle of its undercarriage.

Sparks of unholy coloration and lurid intensity wriggle in there. It's like a metal coral reef in deep space.

Finian lunges between the seats and seizes the yoke from Imogen. He pushes it hard over, trying to slew us around. This has zero effect.

We rise up alongside the boxcar. Its side melts away like mist, and as we float inside. I see that the floor is littered with vehicles ranging from Silicon People gravsleds to *bicycles*, fact o' God, and several classical Area 51-style flying saucers.

I turn to stare desperately out of my window.

All that's out there is blackness.

Treetop has already vanished.

The police cruiser floats in. The wall opaques behind us. There is no sensation of motion, but we all know how the Ghost Train behaves, anyway.

Fletch's (mostly unwanted) adventures continue in the next volume of the *Interstellar Railroad* series, *Supermassive Blackguard.*

DISCOVER THE ADVENTUROUS WORLDS
OF FELIX R. SAVAGE

An exuberant storyteller with a demented imagination, Felix R. Savage specializes in creating worlds so exciting, you'll never want to leave.

Join the Savage Stories newsletter to get notified of new releases and chances to win free books:

felixrsavage.com/signup

THE SOL SYSTEM RENEGADES SERIES

Near-Future Hard Science Fiction

A genocidal AI is devouring our solar system. Can a few brave men and women save humanity?

In the year 2288, humanity stands at a crossroads between space colonization and extinction. Packed with excitement, heartbreak, and unforgettable characters, the Sol System Renegades series tells a sweeping tale of struggle and deliverance.

Crapkiller
The Galapagos Incident
The Vesta Conspiracy
The Mercury Rebellion
The Luna Deception
The Phobos Maneuver
The Mars Shock
The Callisto Gambit

Keep Off The Grass (short story)
A Very Merry Zero-Gravity Christmas (short story)

THE RELUCTANT ADVENTURES
OF
FLETCHER CONNOLLY
ON THE
INTERSTELLAR RAILROAD

Near-Future Non-Hard Science Fiction

An Irishman in space. Untold hoards of alien technological relics waiting to be discovered. What could possibly go wrong?

Skint Idjit
Intergalactic Bogtrotter
Banjaxed Ceili
Supermassive Blackguard

FIRST CONTACT, INC.

Not A User's Manual

The alien rulers of the galaxy are pyramid marketers, and humanity's role in the grand scam is to play the sucker at the bottom.

Unless we can find suckers of our own to prey on ...

Against The Rules
Payback